THE WEDDING

MARION BEAVERS

WinePress Publishing
MUKILTEO, WA 98275

The Wedding
Copyright © 1997 by Marion C. Beavers

Published by WinePress Publishing
PO Box 1406
Mukilteo, WA 98275

Cover by **DENHAM**DESIGN, Everett, WA

Printed in the United States of America.

Library of Congress Catalog Card Number: 96-61785
ISBN 1-883893-83-6

CONTENTS

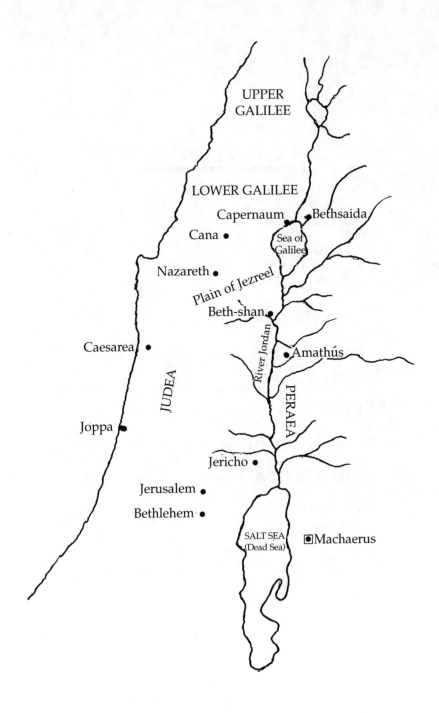

UPPER
GALILEE

LOWER GALILEE

Capernaum • Bethsaida

Cana •

Sea of
Galilee

Nazareth •

Plain of Jezreel

Beth-shan •

River Jordan

Caesarea •

Amathús •

JUDEA

PERAEA

Joppa •

Jericho •

Jerusalem •

Bethlehem •

SALT SEA
(Dead Sea)

◉ Machaerus

CHAPTER ONE

Time was running short. The fourteen-year-old Hebrew girl quickly but lovingly smoothed out the piece of embroidered linen, rolled it up, and tied it with a length of narrow emerald-green silk. She knew she must hasten to deliver it to her father's sandal-making shop in their home town of Cana in time to give it to a friend headed for Judea. He would visit Bethlehem in the course of his journey and had promised to give the gift to her closest friend there, along with the news of her betrothal to Reuben ben David. She had begun the embroidery—a beautiful white lily—as soon as the betrothal contract had been agreed upon six months previous, and she hoped her friend would be pleased with it and with the exciting news.

"You had better be off, Miriam," called her mother from downstairs. "Jonas may not wish to be kept waiting. His journey will be long, and he travels more slowly now!"

"I'm ready to leave now, Mama!"

She picked up the roll of linen, wrapped a small towel around it, and flew down the short flight of stairs, stopping to drop a kiss on her mother's cheek as she hastened out the door.

Walking briskly down the dusty road, Miriam reflected how she and her friend, Rebecca, would often sit on the rocks at the foot of the bare hills near Jerusalem after their chores were completed, confiding their innermost feelings, hopes and dreams to each other. They talked of future days when each would marry a handsome young Jewish man and would have her very own home, surrounded by exotic flowers and facing the eastern gate of Jerusalem.

Now that was over, since Miriam's family had moved away, hoping to escape the cruelty of so many Roman soldiers assigned to the area.

"I cannot bear the way the soldiers look at you, Miriam," her father would say. "You are beautiful, you know."

Miriam blushed. "Thank you, Papa. But I still don't want to move!"

"Then consider Jacob, your own brother. You've seen how closely they crack their whips to him as he plays by the road. Should we wait until one rips his back open?" He added that Romans would be in other areas, but not the large number assigned to the temple city of Jerusalem and its surrounding villages.

Nathan ben-Joseph and his wife, Esther, had taken their children, Miriam and Jacob—along with their few worldly possessions—to Cana, a village in Galilee. There was no sandal-maker nearby, and Nathan was expert at the trade. Ten-year-old Jacob was being trained as an apprentice, though his awkward attempts often exasperated his sometimes short-tempered father.

They would make a living in this new place, thought Nathan. He had purchased two fields, one for a vineyard and the other for raising grain. Life would be hard, they realized, but they put their trust in God to sustain them. They had the good fortune to have never gone hungry, in spite of famines. God had seen them through. How impersonal were the pagan gods the Romans and other heathen worshiped. But their God, Elohim, had proven himself in the days of the wilderness wanderings and to the prophet Elijah on Mount Carmel. What had those other gods done? Nathan asked himself. He was a religious man and meditated upon this often.

Miriam continued on to her father's shop, running to follow a yellow butterfly as it fluttered zigzag fashion. Her dark hair was damp at the back of her neck, and curly tendrils escaped her long braids, softly framing her face. The temperature was already rising, and beads of perspiration covered her narrow nose and high forehead. She was breathless when she arrived, for she knew that the villager should be leaving for his journey.

Short, stocky, elderly Jonas was already there, talking with Nathan, and he smiled when Miriam ran through the doorway. She gasped with relief to find him still waiting, and his eyes sparkled with admiration for the slender, olive-skinned girl—so obviously budding into young womanhood. Her beautiful wide brown eyes, rimmed with long black lashes, reminded him of the child he had lost years ago. He turned to swallow a lump in his throat.

"You have a present for me to deliver, little one?" he asked, returning his gaze to her. "And a message of your good news?"

"Yes, Jonas," she answered shyly. "Will it be too much trouble?"

"No, my young friend," he assured her, with his wide mouth displaying a winsome smile. "I know young Rebecca, and it will be my pleasure to do something for you. You often bring me cakes which your mother has baked, and fresh cheeses also. I wish there were more favors I could do for you."

His brown robe of sackcloth, mended in many places, bespoke a man of little means; but his unshaven face was strong, and his eyes were clear and direct. Miriam and her family had befriended this neighbor, who often helped them in their fields.

"I've heard much talk of the Baptist, the one they call John," he said, directing his remarks to Nathan. "While I'm down near Jericho, I thought I'd seek him out and hear what he is saying. He seems to stick mainly to the wilderness, but he is beginning to have many followers. Some come merely out of curiosity, but others wonder if he is the Messiah. I don't agree, and he himself denies it. I'll be interested to hear him, however."

"Don't be a fool and waste your time!" barked Nathan, his face reddening and his normally bent frame straightening somewhat in his anger. "He's nothing but a rabble-rouser, preying on the minds of the illiterate. I wouldn't give him the satisfaction of counting me in his group of listeners!"

Jonas merely smiled—deepening the numerous creases in his face—shook his friend's hand and departed, turning once to hold up the roll of linen and give Miriam an assuring wink as he strode off in the direction of his destination.

'Papa, what is wrong with John the Baptist?" asked Miriam, turning to her father with sober expression. "Why is it so bad to just listen to him?"

Nathan wiped his hands on his long, grubby apron and sat down on the crude wooden bench beside his work table. He smelled of goat hide, oil, and sweat, but his bearded face was kind. Pushing back a lock of thick black hair from his forehead, he looked at his beloved daughter thoughtfully for a moment.

"My dear Mim," as he was wont to call her, "it's so difficult for you to understand some of these things. You have been sheltered from much," he explained, reaching out to pat her hand. "But the men in the village often tell news when we meet in the evenings after dinner. As various ones return from their travels in Judea and Galilee and sometimes other places farther away, they share with us what is going on that would interest us. Much has been said about this man named John, whom they call the Baptist. He urges repentance of sins and immersion in water as a sign of this repentance." He paused and added, "He claims to be preparing the way for Messiah. It simply can't be true! Why, he is a wild man—shouting, dressed poorly, hurling insults."

"Preparing the way for Messiah?" exclaimed Miriam, her eyes opening wide.

"Yes, and he says nothing about the priests offering sacrifices...the age-old custom we follow. And furthermore, he calls us a generation of vipers. What do you think of that?"

"It sounds like strange talk, Papa. Messiah is supposed to come as a king. Surely Jonas won't believe this man, will he?"

"Jonas is pretty level-headed, of course, but it will be a pure waste of valuable time. Oh well, maybe I was too quick to anger."

Nathan's dark eyes rested on her face, and his expression softened as he looked at her. These two enjoyed talking together, and she was often curious about current happenings. She realized that he conversed with her more than most fathers would. He asserted that he greatly believed in the development and use of any young mind and disliked custom holding her back in any way as far as her intellect was concerned.

"Run home now, Mim," he ordered, picking up a knife and a piece of goat hide. "I must get back to work and finish this pair of sandals for Irnahash."

Miriam could not keep her thoughts on serious talk today and was glad for the opportunity to leave the odorous shop and return to her house to work on her wedding dress. She was to meet Reuben by the village well when the sun was going down over the mountain to the northwest towards Jotapata. She must hasten to lay the clothes out to dry on the roof for her mother and then do some fine handwork on the bottom of her white linen gown.

As she approached her house, she could not help but feel a sharp pang at the thought of leaving this place which had been her home for two years. The sale of the family house near Jerusalem had enabled Nathan to purchase a small but adequate stone house in Cana which had been vacated. Inside it was paneled with cedar, and the central court was paved with red tiles. A fountain adorned the center of the court, and Esther had surrounded it with pots of palms and seasonal flowers in bloom.

Miriam's room was upstairs. It was small and plain, furnished with only a sleeping mat and a beautifully-carved chest which contained certain items she treasured. Among these was an oil lamp given her by her grandmother, to be used in her own future home. She also kept her wedding gown in this chest, taking it out when time permitted and adding fine embroidery stitches which would draw the attention of all who gazed upon it. Miriam was especially talented in the art of handwork, having been taught by her grandmother before she died.

Her favorite spot in the whole house was the roof. She loved to go up there in the cool of evening to sit on a cushion and look out over the surrounding country-side. There was no house directly adjoining theirs, and Miriam was grateful for this. Although she loved friends and enjoyed the companionship of others, she was a private person at times and often enjoyed being alone with her thoughts and prayers.

Her whole family assembled on the roof when the day's work was completed. It was a time of evening worship and quiet communion with one another. Those hours on the roof were usually times of learning more about God.

Now Miriam took a sentimental look about her and called to her mother as she came through the gate. She inhaled the tantalizing smell of freshly-baked bread, giving her a warm and comfortable feeling. She loved her home and family and felt especially close to her mother. Esther had wanted more children, but after Jacob was born, her womb was barren. It was only natural that the mother and daughter would be close.

Esther was wringing out the washing and turned to look at Miriam coming across the courtyard. The mother's face was serene despite the lines beginning to etch themselves at the corners of her wide brown eyes and along the sides of her full mouth. She stood straight and tall, despite hard work, and she looked younger than her thirty-five years. Her luxuriant dark brown hair was drawn back tightly in a bun at the nape of her neck, and she presented a gracious figure as she smiled warmly at Miriam.

"Miriam, dear, did you find Jonas in time to give him Rebecca's gift?" she asked in a well-modulated voice. She added, "It would be nice to have Rebecca as one of your wedding attendants."

"Yes, Mama, I shall. And Jonas was still at the shop when I arrived. Papa got in a bit of a tiff when he heard Jonas say he was going to hear John the Baptist, but he was all right when I left. You know how he gets sometimes."

"Oh, yes, how well I know, my dear, but he always gets over it. I hope you weren't hostile to your father. That would not please either one of us."

"Oh, no, Mama. I was nice to him. I merely asked him a question, and he settled down quickly. He's sort of like an animal that likes to growl one minute and rub his head against you the next." She bent down to smell the newly-baked bread, sniffing and breaking off a piece with a smile.

"That's about right," Esther said with a laugh, as she wrung out the last piece of clothing. "These clothes are ready to be laid out on the roof now. You came home just in time."

Miriam picked up the basket and took it up to the roof, quickly spreading the washing out in the bright sun to dry. She lifted her voice in a song from the Psalms, praising God for putting such joy in her heart. Nothing must mar her happiness now, for in six months she would become the bride of Reuben...the friend she had adored from childhood. Although he was four years her senior, she had often followed him around for no reason at all but to be with him. If he became annoyed and chastised her for it, she soon found out that a few tears on her part would bring him to her side...for a while. Later, as both realized that new emotions were stirring inside them, they each became shy and slowly grew apart.

Their parents had been close friends for many years, both in Jerusalem and now in Cana. It was almost as if they were destined to become betrothed.

Now Miriam ran down the stairs from the roof and up another shorter flight to reach her own room.

I must use all of my skill on this beautiful gown, she resolved, as she tenderly removed the white linen garment, wrapped in a sheet of cloth to keep it spotless. I so want Reuben to think me beautiful in it, she mused, laying it out on her sleeping mat and making sure the cloth protected it. I wonder what he will wear? He will be handsome, even if he wears goat hide...but of course, it will be something colorful and elegant.

Miriam was washing the dishes after the evening meal when she realized that her time to meet Reuben was at hand. She ran outside to empty the dishwater and then bathed and donned a fresh pink linen robe.

13

The sun was going down over the mountains and the sky had turned a golden pink hue in the west as she slipped into the new sandals her father had made for her. Kissing her mother and father, she headed for the nearby village well. She and Reuben liked to meet there, as they could talk alone for the brief period of time she was allowed to stay. She must be back home when family worship began and before it became dark.

Papa is always on time, she reflected. He insists that we never waste a moment, since time is so precious. Sometime I would enjoy wasting a whole day!

The tall and lithe Reuben was waiting for her when she arrived at the well. As usual, their meeting was awkward at first. Inasmuch as their betrothal had been announced six months previous, both families had recently agreed that it was fitting that they know one another better. The couple had discreetly been staying away from each other ever since their future had been sealed by their fathers.

"Shalom, Miriam," Reuben said with a boyish grin. "I like your pretty robe. The color is right for you."

"Thank you, Reuben," she replied, a blush rising in her smiling face. "How did your day go?" What was there really to talk about? she considered anxiously.

"I worked in the vineyard," he replied nervously, as if he wanted to say something but didn't know how. "My father said he needed me more there than in the shop."

His eyes took in her glowing ones and glanced downward at her slim but developing figure. He moved closer to her until he could reach out and grasp her slender fingers, and hers responded and wound around his. A thrill went through her whole body, as if an awakening were taking place. He seemed to feel the same, for they both turned so that their dark eyes met. Reuben's handsome and clean-shaven face shone as he smiled down at her.

"You are very pretty," he said softly. "I'm glad our families arranged for us to be betrothed. After knowing you when we were children, it's hard to believe we will soon be married. Such a short time ago we were playmates and now we are..." He wasn't certain how to finish what he was saying.

"We are what, Reuben?" she questioned, smiling sweetly with anticipation.

"Well, I guess you would say we are...lovers. Isn't that what we are when we are betrothed?

"I guess so," she ventured, as a thrill went down her spine. "It sounds nice, anyway. I don't know much about lovers, but I suppose that's what we are." Her eyelids dropped down, and she stared at her feet.

"Doesn't it mean I can kiss you?" Reuben asked shyly but with a certain eagerness, as he looked at her soft red mouth.

"I've never had anyone but my family kiss me," she replied, looking back up into his eyes, "but aren't we family now?"

"Yes, we must be," he answered as he bent his head slowly and uncertainly, very gently touching her lips with his and quickly drawing away lest he be too forward.

His very touch stirred Miriam with an awareness she had never had. Even with her attraction to Reuben, she had never felt the ecstasy of physical contact with him. It was brief, but it sent a little electric current through her.

"That was nice, Reuben. I didn't mind it at all," she said reservedly.

Then he put his arms around her waist and kissed her again…a little longer. As he drew away, both looked deep and long into each other's eyes.

"I must go now," she said with reluctance, and turned and ran towards home.

Reuben stood for awhile, watching this lovely nymph-like creature until she was home and out of sight. He touched his lips with his fingers and wondered about it all, feeling deeply stirred within.

Miriam's mind wandered during the evening worship and family conversation that evening. She still relived her first moment of rapture with Reuben and feared that her family would notice a difference in her face and eyes. Her brother, Jacob, irritated her by staring at her with an impish grin on his face. She turned away and looked up at the multitude of stars shining in the heavens, pretending to have her thoughts on them.

The stars appeared brighter tonight than usual, and they seemed to be singing a song to her as they blinked. However, two shining brown eyes outshone them all in her consciousness. She considered little else except the thrill which remained on her lips and in her breast. She already knew that she loved the young man she was to marry. He was not only pleasing to look upon—with his lean muscular physique, his dark brown, wavy hair and his kind dark eyes—but he was also a gentle and caring person. How could she be so blessed? She had long admired him.

Miriam and Reuben did not meet at the well the following evening, as Reuben's parents—David and Johhebed—had invited Nathan, Esther, Miriam and

Jacob to dine with them, saying they had interesting news to relate. Both families had been the closest of friends over the years and had shared many meals, so no special significance was given to this one. Their homes were situated fairly close together, so distance presented no problem. David and Johhebed had just returned from Jerusalem, where they too had previously lived. David had obtained some camel's hide for Nathan's shop. David himself did special carving on furniture and ornaments and had sought out particular wood on his journey. He fashioned many objects of olive wood, as well as tools of hardwood. Both fathers were training their sons in their respective trades.

"Greetings, my good friend," said David, embracing Nathan as the family arrived at his home. "It's good to be back at Cana, especially to see you again. Things are much more peaceful here."

"And good to see you too, David," agreed Nathan warmly, returning the embrace. Standing back and eyeing his friend, Nathan added with a chuckle, "Do I notice a slight addition of weight to your husky frame? No doubt you feasted well on your journey!"

The portly man pulled in his abdomen and countered, "Pure imagination, Nathan. It is your vision," he assured him with a twinkle in his eye.

With the rest of the family following, the men entered the rock-paved court and then the inner court where a table was surrounded by colorful cushions. They enjoyed eating outdoors when the weather was pleasant. Reuben had a younger sister, Rhoda, a spirited young girl of ten. She was a smaller copy of Johhebed, tall and slight of frame, with a rather pointed chin and nose, thin lips and wide almond-shaped eyes. There was an impish quality about both Rhoda and Johhebed, which made up for their lack of actual beauty. Being of happy dispositions, their frequent smiles enhanced their physical appeal.

"I have a lot to tell you," said Rhoda to Miriam as the two girls helped serve the meal. "Mama says we can go to my room later."

"Oh, that will be fine," answered Miriam politely, while glancing at Reuben out of the corner of her eye. Surely he and she would be given time to talk later. Rhoda was still a little girl, and Miriam considered herself a grown young woman—now that she was nubile and betrothed as well.

The meal began with hot lentil soup flavored with leeks and garlic, followed by servings of goat meat, cucumbers, bread and wine. An atmosphere of conviviality prevailed among the friends until David suddenly stood up after all had finished eating.

"I have something important to tell you," he announced.

Conversation subsided, and the guests sat up straight on their cushions, anxious to hear the latest bit of news. A mockingbird trilled a message to his mate in the otherwise quiet surroundings.

David stroked his well-trimmed black beard, assumed a serious manner, and after giving his wife a knowing look, turned to Nathan.

"We had an opportunity several times to hear John, the one they call the Baptist, when we journeyed to the zor of the lower Jordan Valley. We have been greatly touched by his message. We feel his sincerity and wisdom, and we're giving much thought to what he has to say. As you know, he is a cousin of Johhebed."

A heavy silence filled the place, as if no one had the power to speak. Only the shrill cry of a night hawk could be heard. Miriam seemed turned to stone as she riveted her wide eyes on her father's face, fearing what his reaction would be. Esther too looked at her husband anxiously, knowing his negative opinion of the Baptist. Reuben lowered his head, not wanting to look at anyone. Only Johhebed smiled gently at her husband in support of his pronouncement.

"He made much sense," she whispered softly to Esther, "and we only wish you could hear him also. We can hardly wait to return to the lower Jordan Valley so that we can hear him again. Many people of all walks of life come."

Esther returned a vague smile, but Nathan's face was turning red. It was evident he could contain himself no longer.

"Impossible!" he roared. "Simply impossible that you—our dear friends of a lifetime—would fall prey to the words of such a rabble-rouser who lives in the dense brush of the wilderness and is said to live on nothing but carob pods—mere cattle food—and wild honey! People say he looks like a barbarian, unshaven and dressed in clothing made from camel hair. My apologies, Johhebed," he inserted, turning to her, "but your cousin does not reflect upon you." Returning his gaze to David, he continued. "What special wisdom could he have concerning God's word? We have the Holy Scriptures available in the synagogues. What more do we need? Even the Essenes, that sect at Qumran are copying them word for word." His face was livid and contorted by now, and Esther eyed him anxiously.

Johhebed's face reddened, but she remained silent. David was unruffled, however, and suggested, "Let us speak of other things now, my friend. I did not mean to upset you so. I merely wanted to share something which has become important to us. By the way," he added as a means of changing the subject, "Reuben is going to Nazareth this week on an errand for me. A young carpenter, Jesus—another cousin of Johhebed, in fact—is in need of a very special tool which I have made. Reuben will carry it to him. Is there something he can get you in that area? He will stop by to see Jesus' mother also...she is widowed. We've been too busy since moving here to visit them, but we must make up for lost time by inviting them to the wedding. It's not good to neglect our relatives."

"No, thank you," Nathan curtly replied, and rose to take his family home. Miriam was devastated and turned to look pleadingly at Reuben. He gave her a solemn wink to assure her he understood, and she followed her family out the door after they thanked David and Johhebed for the meal.

The walk home was made in silence.

CHAPTER TWO

A nxiety filled Miriam's heart the following day. She had been trained always to respect her father and his feelings, but she could only anticipate trouble because of David's pronouncement. She and Esther did not mention the incident but went about their daily tasks as if nothing had happened, except for a quiet uneasiness. Would the time never come for her to meet Reuben at the well? Even keeping busy with the many household chores and her embroidery work could not dispel this disquietude. Her heart was heavy in her breast, and her eyes were glazed with a look of anxiety. She had a distinct feeling of foreboding.

When Nathan wearily returned home from the day's work, his face was a mask of serious introspection, and he said little during the meal hour. He had carried some bread and fruit to the shop with him for his noontime meal, so the family had not seen him all day long.

The time finally arrived for Miriam to leave. She came downstairs dressed in a robe of yellow linen tied with a brown girdle and hesitantly went over to plant a kiss on her father's cheek, putting her arm around his shoulder.

"I'll be back soon, Papa, and will join you on the roof for prayers. You, too, Mama," she added, stepping lightly over to embrace her mother. Her promise was needless, she knew, for she always returned on time, but she needed to say something to break the awkward silence.

"Yes, Miriam," Esther answered with a gentle smile. But Nathan said nothing. He merely glanced at her with a thoughtful look in his eyes, his forehead creased as if attempting to think out a problem.

Miriam turned soberly and went out through the gate with a heavier step than usual. Trouble in the family never came easy for her, having been reared in an atmosphere of love and caring. She understood her father's stubbornness and quick temper, but these were usually transitory. Although there was no active dissension today, a tenseness in the atmosphere indicated that all was not well. No breeze stirred, and the stifling heat of the day hung heavily. She wished for rain. As she walked toward the well, her sandals were already dusty from the road. Nothing seemed right…until she came to the well where the familiar and beloved figure waited for her.

"Oh, Miriam, I thought you would never come—even though you are not late," Reuben exclaimed, running his fingers through his black, wavy hair. "This has been a very long day for me…waiting to see you." He grasped hold of her hand and put his other hand on her shoulder.

"It has been an eternity for me, Reuben. How do you feel after last evening?" she asked, looking up into his eyes.

"I don't know how to feel, if you're talking about father's mention of John the Baptist, and your father's reaction. As for me, I missed meeting you here last evening."

"I was talking about our fathers, but I missed meeting you too."

"Let's not worry about our families, Miriam," he suggested, giving her shoulder and hand a slight squeeze and smiling wistfully into her face. "I want to talk about you and me now."

Miriam lowered her eyes, and Reuben continued to look upon her face and the long dark lashes which rested on her smooth cheeks.

"What do you want to say about us?" Miriam asked softly, looking once more into his eyes that were tenderly devouring hers.

He stammered, "I just want to let you know that I...I...love you!" Lowering his head and wiping his perspiring brow he added, "There...I've said it...and I mean it!"

"Oh, Reuben," Miriam answered with feeling. "I love you too. I knew it when I was on our roof looking at the stars last night. I knew I really loved you."

Reuben took hold of her dimpled chin, raised it upwards and slowly and tenderly placed his lips on hers. Miriam responded slightly, just enough to let him know that she belonged to him and that one day she would be wholly his. This was her desire of all desires. Her kiss was a seal of approval and hope for a marriage blessed of God. His arms went around her waist in an embrace, and then he let her go. She was his beloved, and he was hers. That was all that mattered now.

"I must go," she whispered, and turned for home, glancing back once to give him a wave of her hand and a smile. The day had ended well. Why should I worry one bit more about Papa and his sharp words to David?.

Miriam sat through the family worship hour with a peace in her soul and a heart swelling with love. Strange feelings began to manifest themselves inside her body, and she wondered if she might be coming down with some new malady. But no illness would be this pleasant and so filled with excitement, she reflected. She could actually feel her eyes sparkle and it was all she could do to keep from shouting with joy.

"Mim, why do you refrain from bowing your head as we pray?" her father asked her. "Could it be that you do not have your mind on God?"

She quickly bowed her head, filled with embarrassment and remorse for being so inattentive at prayer time. As Nathan's praises and entreaties went up to the throne of God, she kept her mind on every word, not wanting to be found lacking by the Almighty. She both loved and feared God, and she hated herself for her recent mental journeys during the hours of worship. She would have much to confess on the Day of Atonement.

Nathan decided the following morning to walk over to David's shop to pick up the camel hide David had brought back from his journey to Judea. Cana was not on a popular trade route, but Judea—particularly around Jerusalem and Bethelehem—abounded in merchants. Thus, bargaining for lower prices was prevalent. It was more expedient to go there for the wood and leather they desired…not to mention the opportunity to buy silks, spices and objects of art. Nathan and David did not aspire to, nor could they afford, many of the exotic items, but it was exciting for the women to look and dream of such things.

David had brought back some cedar from this last trip and was sawing and fitting the pieces into the making of a small chest which a prominent citizen had ordered. It was to have intricate carving on the drawers, and that is where David excelled.

"Peace be unto you, David," said Nathan, more reserved in manner than usual as he entered the shop which smelled strongly of cedar. Nathan kicked aside some wood chips from the floor.

"And unto you!" answered David warmly, wiping his hands on a soiled towel before embracing his friend. "What brings you away from your own busy shop? I gather Jacob is tending to things for you?"

"Yes. I left him cutting strips of hide. That is one thing he can do on his own…providing he doesn't cut off the end of a finger in the process. He's a rather clumsy youth at times, but he's trying. I came to pick up the camel hide you brought me and to pay for it. I'm most grateful for your kindness in bringing it to me."

"Do not speak of it, my friend," urged David, sensing a coolness on the part of Nathan. "Have you not often done the same for me when we both lived in Judea and you would journey over to Tyre or Sidon to meet the merchant ships? You struck some good bargains in those days," he recalled with a smile. He strode to a corner of the sawdust-littered shop and picked up a large bundle tied with rope. Hoisting it onto his burly shoulder, he brought it to Nathan.

"This wasn't a bad bargain, either. The merchant was tired and obviously eager to rid himself of the smelly hide, so it was not difficult to arrive at a fair price. We took our cart, of course, and it was little or no problem for us. It's always good to do you a favor, you know. I'm happy to help a friend."

Nathan relieved him of the strong smelling bundle, paid him the price marked on it, but did not leave the shop immediately. Dropping the hide down on a nearby work table, he seated himself on a crudely-made bench, hunching his shoulders and placing a broad, rough hand on each thigh.

"I think we have to talk, David," he said in a tone which brought a sober look to his friend's face.

"Something is bothering you, Nathan. Is it what I said about going to hear John the Baptizer when we were in Jordan?"

"You know very well that is what is bothering me. I can't understand you, David. You have always been a man of faith. You have gone regularly to the synagogue. You keep the law of Moses...as well as any of us can keep it. You are raising your family in the fear and admonition of the Lord. Then this! It's a sacrilege! An abomination to God! What happened to you?"

Pulling up a small wooden box beside Nathan, David sat down and looked at him lovingly and said, "Nothing has happened to me, Nathan. I still love God. I still try to keep the law. I still go to the synagogue. But the man makes sense, Nathan. He's a godly man, too. He worships our God. Johhebed says his father was a high priest."

"Maybe so, but how could an uneducated, uncouth person such as he ever make a carob of sense? That's what I want to know!" thundered Nathan his face becoming red and his eyes flashing.

"These are not things of the intellect, my friend," explained David evenly, obviously trying to remain calm. "These are things of the soul. The man is trying to expose us as we really are. He is showing us that we cannot possibly keep all the law of Moses—that it is humanly impossible to do so because of our inherent nature—and that we need to repent of our sins. He blames us for becoming complacent in our self-righteous attitudes—that we think that because we attend worship in the synagogue and say our prayers, we are divorced from sin."

"He lies!" Nathan roared, waving an arm in the air. "How do we sin—we who live a good life, try hard to work and raise and feed our families, worship and keep the holy days? Just what kind of sins is he talking about?"

"He calls it hypocrisy," answered David, beginning to lose his gentle attitude and becoming slightly louder himself. He said that if one has two coats, he should give one to the man who has none. And we should divide our food with the poor, also. He even claims he is making way for the Messiah himself."

"Hmpff!" snorted Nathan. "I've heard about the Messiah business, though I don't believe this man could possibly know who he is or that the Messiah would have anything to do with him. This man is all but a beggar, and the Messiah will come in glory and rescue us from the Roman yoke. He will be a king! As for the food and clothing, John probably wants it for himself. No, David," he continued, "I have always respected you, but this time I think you are totally wrong—if not a bit addled in the head." To be truthful, I'd rather not speak of it again. I'll take my leave now," he said, rising from the bench and hoisting the bundle of hide to his shoulder.

"Please don't leave in anger, Nathan. I have nothing against you, for you are my dear friend. I do urge you, however, to listen to me further at another time about this man, John. He does speak with a certain authority which I cannot describe. Great crowds are coming to hear him and to be baptized by him."

"I said I want to hear no more about it," Nathan said simply, and strode out of the shop with his bundle of hide.

David watched the familiar figure stride deliberately down the dusty road toward his own shop, his frame bent from constantly leaning over his workbench. David's eyes were moist as he realized the closed-mindedness of his friend. He considered that he too might have reacted in the same manner had he not heard the powerful and soul-rending words of the man in the wilderness.

Miriam did not see her father until he returned from his shop that day. She was helping Esther prepare the evening meal and was thinking about the brief but beautiful moments shared with Reuben the evening before. Her heart soared wildly as she remembered their profession of love for one another, and she sloshed the wine as she poured it from the earthen jar into a clay cup.

"Miriam, you seem to have your mind elsewhere," chided Esther good-naturedly as she neatly arranged the fresh figs and grapes in a bowl. "You have already cut too much cheese, and now you are spilling the wine. Is something bothering you?"

"No, Mama. I was thinking of my love for Reuben and how I wish I could be with him more."

"Custom forbids it, my daughter. The rabbi insists, even though the laws say you are man and wife once the betrothal contract is sealed."

"I do not understand," replied Miriam, raising her black eyebrows and looking up at her mother.

Esther wiped her hands on a towel and turned to her daughter. Her eyes were compassionate, and her expression serious.

"Miriam, child, there are many things about laws and customs we do not understand. But God in his wisdom put them in the heart of Moses—often spoke outright to him—and we must accept what God decrees. Your father and I, along with David and Johhebed, have been most lenient in letting you and Rueben meet for a few moments each evening by the well. We thought much about this before we let you do it, but we could not help but feel you would have a better beginning with your marriage than your father and I did," Esther explained, putting her hands lovingly on Miriam's arms.

"I'm grateful to you for this, Mama. But tell me about your marriage...the beginning part, I mean. Was it not good? I always thought..."

"Oh, it was good in many ways, my daughter," Esther interrupted, "but I was so terribly shy and afraid. You see, I hardly knew your father, and he wanted to make love to me at every opportunity. It was something I knew nothing about. I had never even kissed a man, of course. He seemed wildly obsessed with me."

"You are a beautiful woman, Mama. I can understand why Papa would love you. You are sweet and gentle, too," Miriam added, tears welling close to the surface of her eyes. Her mother was very dear to her.

They were both startled out of their close communion by the heavy stride of Nathan approaching the doorway. As they saw his troubled face, the two women were instantly aware that something was wrong.

"What has happened, my husband?" exclaimed Esther, walking over and embracing him warmly. "You do not come home in your usual happy manner. Something is disturbing you."

"I lost my temper with David this morning, and departed with ill will in my heart," he answered, returning her embrace while maintaining a distant and hardened expression. "I seek his forgiveness, but the issue remains the same."

At the mention of David, Miriam tensed and stopped ladling out the soup. Her thoughts raced to the harsh words spoken by her father two evenings previous, and she had an uneasy feeling that the issue he mentioned was that one.

"What issue, Nathan?" questioned Esther in a barely audible voice as she looked into his troubled eyes.

"About John the Baptist!" he bellowed, unable to constrain himself longer. Why can't Esther understand? Why doesn't she leave the matter alone and not question me?

"But, why?..." Miriam started to say more, but knew she must not openly disagree with her father.

Nathan shot her a quick glance, as if he dared her to show him disrespect, and then turned and shuffled up the stairs to the sanctuary of his bedroom.

"Put the soup on," Esther instructed Miriam as she followed her husband upstairs. "I'll be down in a few moments."

Miriam's heart pounded and a knot began to form in her stomach. Her hands shook as she set the soup out.

She was thankful no one was nearby to observe her reaction to her father's outburst. Anything affecting Reuben's family now affected her.

Why should Papa be so upset? Do not the Holy Scriptures tell us to mind our own business and not interfere with others? It's not as if David were a heathen. He has not given himself over to another god.

Nathan descended the stairs and strode into the kitchen, interrupting her thoughts.

"Where is Jacob?" he asked harshly. "The soup will be cold if he does not come."

"Here I am, Papa," said the gangly boy, coming quickly into the kitchen behind his mother and quickly washing his face and hands in the basin sitting on a small stand. "I've been watching a viper stalk its prey on the side of the house. It was only after a cankerworm, which we can easily do without. Mmmm, the soup smells good."

Nathan and Jacob entered the dining room and stood at their usual places as Esther and Miriam brought in the wine, cheese, bread and bowl of fruit. All remained still with bowed heads as Nathan asked God's blessings on the food and the household in his deep, rich voice which shook a bit today.

The meal was eaten in silence, broken only once by Jacob, who asked a trivial question about the shop. He seemed to sense the tension too and nervously tried to break it with small talk, not knowing the real problem.

Nathan remained deep in thought, and the family knew to leave him alone. They were familiar with these occasional moods of his and knew he was pondering a matter of importance. Miriam turned to Esther with a questioning look and was disturbed at the anxious expression in her mother's eyes. A tear slid slowly down Esther's cheek, but she was compelled to remain silent until Nathan spoke.

Why does it have to be this way? Miriam yearned to go to her father and put her arms around him, to try and comfort him. But this was not to be done. They must wait until he broke the silence—if he did.

Finally, Nathan pushed his plate away and looked around at each member of his family. "I have come to a decision. I shall go to see the rabbi tonight."

"I see," said Esther. "Are you sure this is what you wish to do?"

"Yes. I see no other way." He rose from the table without another word and left the house, striding down the road.

"Mama," asked Miriam in a trembling voice, "why is Papa going to see the rabbi?"

"I don't know how to tell you this, my child, without hurting you. But your father is considering breaking the betrothal contract if David and Johhebed continue to follow John the Baptist."

Miriam weakened as if she had been dealt a blow, and she felt almost faint. She groped for the work table to steady herself and her face paled.

"But why, Mama?" she asked, gaining strength as anger flowed through her. "We have already pledged ourselves to one another. We love each other. It makes no difference to us if David and Johhebed choose to follow the man, John. Reuben and I will live our own lives, and I will follow the things you and Papa have taught me. Reuben is a devout Jew. He has shown no interest at all in that man!"

Miriam paled again as she considered the impact of her father's reactions and his visit to the rabbi. Rabbi Elishua was a reasonable and kind man, but he was also known for his strict adherence to every jot and tittle of Jewish law. The Torah was his very lifeblood, and he tolerated no deviation from it. This could amount to a devastating turn of events for her and Reuben, she realized with trepidation.

Hustling to clear the table and wash up the dishes, she ran up to her room and changed into a pale blue tunic, tying it around the waist with a darker blue girdle. The blue seemed to bring out her clear olive skin and dark brown hair and eyes. It was time to leave to meet Reuben, and she needed him more than ever tonight. Not a moment must be wasted in their brief encounter together, for he was to leave for Nazareth in the morning and would not return for several days. She needed his confidence that nothing would prevent their marriage, although deep down in her heart she knew that her father would make the final decision. This was the patriarchal way of life for the Jewish people, and she was not to question it.

Bolting down the stairs, she almost collided with her brother as she headed for the courtyard, where Esther was watering the plants she favored so highly. Each new leaf or bud was exciting to her, and she often spoke aloud to them.

"Watch where you're going!" admonished Jacob. "Can't wait to see Reuben, eh? You're no fun anymore since you got betrothed to him."

"Be quiet, Jacob!" Miriam retorted. "Just wait until you grow up. You won't want to play childish games either."

Ignoring the tongue stuck out at her, she ran out to kiss her mother gently on the cheek, promising to return at the usual time, as she fled through the gate. She saw Reuben standing by the well a short distance away, and her breath caught in her throat for a moment, causing her to gasp. He was so handsome and strong. The work with his father and in the fields had developed his body and given his face a ruddy color. He fairly glowed as he watched her come down the road, kicking an occasional rock aside on the way. He laughed heartily as an insect landed on her and she brushed it off frantically. She laughed back, and then she was with him.

"Oh, Reuben," she said immediately, as he took her small hands in his long, slim fingers. "Much has happened, and we must talk quickly!"

"Something is wrong, Miriam. I can tell by your face. Whatever has happened?" He cupped her chin in his hand and turned her face up to look more closely in her eyes.

"Don't you know?" Didn't your father mention that my father and he had a disagreement about John the Baptist today and that Papa left in anger?"

"No, he didn't say anything in front of me. Come to think of it, he did look preoccupied. But, why should that cause you to frown so?"

"Because...because...Reuben, Papa has gone to see the rabbi about it. He's there now, and he is thinking of breaking our betrothal!"

"Breaking our betrothal?" Reuben's dark eyes widened, and his mouth fell open in astonishment. "What would that have to do with our betrothal?" He grabbed her hands and squeezed them tightly.

"I don't know," answered Miriam, her eyes filling with tears, "but I know he was in earnest by the way he stalked out of the house and down the road toward the synagogue with his robe flapping. Oh, Reuben, what are we to do? It doesn't matter to me if your parents follow John the Baptist. You and I are followers of God and the holy laws. Isn't that what matters?"

"It's all that matters to me...and that we love each other," affirmed Reuben, leaning over to plant a light kiss on her forehead. "I must speak with your father as soon as I return from Nazareth. I'm sure I can make him understand."

"Oh, I hope so," answered Miriam, her eyes gazing intensely into his. "But now I must leave. I'll miss you while you're gone. Do be careful on your journey, and watch out for wild beasts and thieves. I'll pray for your safety."

"Thank you, my love. And I'll be thinking of the situation with your father while I'm gone. I know it will work out...somehow."

Reuben took Miriam in his arms and kissed her gently on the lips, then released her. Both turned and walked away to their own homes.

CHAPTER THREE

Nathan had not returned when Miriam joined Esther and Jacob on the roof. It was almost dark and the young woman sat down on her usual cushion, looking up at the feeble light of stars in the sky.

Her mother glanced at her compassionately, but remained silent, knowing that she wished to be alone with her thoughts. The whole situation was difficult for her daughter, Esther mused, for she knew that a broken betrothal would present many problems for Miriam. Perhaps Rabbi Elishua would talk Nathan out of it. He was a reasonable man, although one who taught and preached strict adherence to the law. Esther suddenly felt weary and leaned back against the low wall surrounding the roof, closing her eyes contemplatively.

The moments dragged for both women until they heard Nathan's plodding footsteps on the stairs. Miriam's heart beat faster as she awaited the news he would bring. She became almost excited as she considered the possibility of their beloved rabbi's answer in favor of herself and Reuben. Then it would most likely be settled for all time, inasmuch as her father had the highest respect for the teacher of holy writ.

"Shalom, loved ones," said Nathan solemnly as he dragged his tired feet over to his family, draped his prayer shawl over his shoulders and pulled out a scroll from under his tunic. His eyes held a fixed stare. Jacob awoke from a corner where he had been dozing, and he and the two women greeted Nathan warmly and expectantly. Miriam trembled and swallowed hard as she awaited the words her father would say.

"Tonight we read the words of the psalmist as he agonized over the people's idolatry." He cleared his throat to begin.

Esther could stand the suspense no longer. "But, Nathan,…the rabbi…"

"We shall have time for that later," he responded sternly. "God's word must come first. Then we shall speak of other things."

Miriam's face fell and Esther obediently folded her hands and looked at her husband as he began to read. Stealing a look at her daughter, who was biting her lower lip nervously, Esther predicted that the worship time would be lost on Miriam this evening.

"'We have heard with our ears, O God, our fathers have told us what work you did in their days, in the times of old. How you drove out the heathen with your hand, and planted them; how you afflicted the people and cast them out.

"'For they got not the land in possession by their own sword, neither did their own arm save them; but thy right hand and thine arm....Thou has given us like sheep appointed for meat, and has scattered us among the heathen....You make us a reproach to our neighbors, a scorn and a derision to them that are round about us.'"

The sonorous voice continued with an occasional pause to swallow hard, as if he were about to be overcome by emotion.

"'...if we have forgotten the name of our God or stretched out our hands to a strange god; shall not God search this out? For He knows the secrets of the heart...arise for our help, and redeem us for your mercies' sake.'

"God is telling us, through the psalmist, that we are a disobedient people. He has guided his people through the wilderness, through wars, through prophetic utterances, and through his holy Word, but we still stray and seek other ways, other gods, strange men to lead us. We are a weak people and refuse to be obedient to the law. We deserve his wrath and his punishment. Only when we refuse to digress from strict obedience to him, will we ever find peace and contentment."

Miriam recognized that these words were meant to reflect upon David and Johhebed's interest in John the Baptist.

Nathan then bowed his head to pray, followed by the three members of his family. He rocked back and forth as he petitioned: "O Lord God in heaven, look down upon us, your humble servants, and help us to be more worthy of you. We are surely as nothing in your sight...weak and undeserving. We study your laws and try to keep them, but often we fail. Bring us out from under the bondage of our Roman oppressors, and send the Messiah to rule over us in glory and majesty. Help us to bear up until he comes to bring us peace. Amen."

He then seated himself on a mat and cleared his throat as he looked around at each member of his family in the flickering lamp light that burned brighter now that it was dark.

The full moon cast its silvery beams on their rooftop. The sky was cloudless, and stars were like silver dust as far as the eye could see. Miriam felt that God was almost close enough to touch, although she knew that he was spirit and could not really be touched. She looked at her father expectantly, hoping he would reveal the outcome of his visit to Rabbi Elishua. She was confident it would be favorable news.

"Now I shall tell you about my talk with Rabbi Elishua," Nathan announced in a ponderous and solemn manner. He looked into Esther's eyes and then into Miriam's before continuing.

"He feels, as I do, that John the Baptist is a rabble-rouser and is turning many people away from Moses's law by adding to it with his insistence upon baptism. He claims to be preparing the way for Messiah...our King of kings...while living in the wilderness like a pauper. He is arousing the people to lose respect for our esteemed religious leaders and is preaching things we haven't heard before."

Miriam's face blanched and she felt cold and clammy. Tears welled up inside and she could barely hold them back. She knew what was coming.

"Mim," Nathan said huskily, looking at his daughter, "I have considered this very carefully. I have come to a decision I feel is only right. Since Reuben's parents, our dearest friends, David and Johhebed, insist upon following this man who is indoctrinating so many to a new teaching, I fear that Reuben himself will gradually be drawn into this sect. Then God's wrath could be upon both of you, and I love you too much to have that happen if I can possibly prevent it. The only recourse I can arrive at is to break the betrothal. And that is what I plan to do."

Tears streamed down Miriam's face, as she softly murmured, "Oh, Papa..." She knew her father's word was law in the family, but why couldn't she at least try to convince him that she and Reuben were not drawn to the Baptist and would not follow his teaching? Should she not risk his anger and try? What could she stand to lose? Reuben was all she wanted anyway, and now she was about to lose the one she loved so much.

Falteringly, she looked first at her mother, who sat with head bent, not wishing to face either her husband or her daughter. Then she looked back at her father's troubled but determined face and ventured to say, "Please, Papa, Reuben and I would not follow the Baptist. We have never seen him nor heard him and have no desire to do so. All we want is to be together for the rest or our lives."

Nathan looked at his daughter harshly, softened his expression for a moment, then resumed his stern gaze.

"The decision is made, Mim. Do not attempt to change my mind. Tomorrow I go to see David."

"But Reuben will be in Nazareth tomorrow," said Miriam, in a further attempt to forestall the dreaded pronouncement."

"It is not necessary that Reuben be present," stated Nathan flatly. "We will take care of it in a day or so with the rabbi. Since the actual wedding has not taken place and the marriage therefore not consummated, there should be no problem. The family decision is what counts at this point."

"And Reuben has no say?" asked Miriam in astonishment.

"The rabbi explained what is to be done. Now say no more about it. Let us descend to our rooms for the night. I am very weary. Come, Esther. Wake up, Jacob! You have been dozing again!"

Miriam was the last to leave the roof, feeling that hope was all gone for her. Her throat tightened, and she gazed with yearning in the direction of Reuben's house. If she could only transmit her thoughts to him and let him know what was taking place: Perhaps he could delay his journey a day or so...or maybe I could join him on his journey; and we could keep on going and going...away from all of this. Then the betrothal could not be broken! But how could I be thinking such wild thoughts? What would we live on? Where would we settle? It would do nothing but bring shame to my beloved family. No, that was not the answer, she concluded sadly. But what was the answer?

Miriam was so filled with sorrow that she went to her room and flung herself on her mat, sobbing into her pillow so as not to awaken the others who might be already asleep. Then she heard the agitated voices of her parents. Her father's tones were sharp and audible, but her mother spoke softly, almost in a whisper. It was clear they were arguing. Miriam listened intently, for Nathan and Esther rarely argued. His temper was quick but short-lived, and Esther had a way of controlling the situation in a calm and pacifying manner. However, tonight she did not appear to be in control.

"I have said it over and over, Esther, and none of your honeyed words can change my mind," Miriam heard her father say. "Tomorrow I go to see David. Tonight I wish to get some sleep, for I am very weary. Let's discuss it no further." Then the house was silent and Miriam was left with her inner despair.

"Oh, God of our fathers," she reached out in a whisper, "please help me. You know how much Reuben and I love each other, and we try hard to be obedient to you. Change my father's heart, and let Reuben and me have our wedding. And give Reuben a safe journey tomorrow. Protect him from thieves or other unpleasant persons while on the way, and please watch over him. He is not only my betrothed...he is my true love. I leave him in your hands. Amen."

She hoped her prayer was heard, and soon she fell into a fitful sleep. Just before dawn she was fully awake and ran up to the roof in hope of seeing Reuben leave for Nazareth. As the sun began tinting the horizon a glorious pink and orange, she saw a lone figure walking briskly down the road in the distance and knew it must be her love.

"Oh, Reuben," she said softly, reaching out her arms in his direction, "you cannot know what is happening or you wouldn't leave. Please turn around and come back, Reuben!" But the figure disappeared over a hill and was gone.

Reuben had a song in his heart as he strode up the hill in the southerly direction of Nazareth. He had considered riding a donkey, but his father was in need of the beast to pull his cart when he delivered the chest he had completed.

"Oh, well," he voiced aloud, "the morning air is cool, and the walk will do me good. I am young and strong, and the time will go quickly with my beloved to think about."

"Hosanna to God in the highest!" he sang. His rich baritone voice rang out across the countryside, causing nearby neighbors to run to their door in curiosity.

"Shalom, Aaron, shalom, Huldah!" he shouted to his friends, as he slowed a bit in passing. "Can I bring you something from Nazareth?"

"What is good in Nazareth?" Aaron chided. "No, thank you, Reuben. Go in peace!"

Reuben came to the crest of the hill and descended the other side, out of sight of the village of Cana. It would take him all morning to reach his destination, but he was grateful for the opportunity to be alone and to ponder the troublesome news that Miriam had conveyed to him the previous evening. His was an optimistic nature, however, and he could not believe that Nathan would not listen to reason. *Even the rabbi knows my father's love for God and his obedience to the law and holy days.*

He considered how it had not been long since Purim was celebrated, and his mother had baked the hamentaschen for many of the villagers, including the rabbi and his family. *Why, his father never missed a Sabbath eve at the synagogue, often standing up and reading from the Scriptures.* He was one of the few who read from Isaias of the strange way the Messiah would come, as a lowly babe born in a stable. Rabbi Elishua, on the other hand, always read how he would come in majesty and glory as King of kings. Reuben was confused by this dichotomy but pushed it to the back of his mind for the present. He must mentally prepare what words he would say to Nathan when he returned to Cana. He could not bear the thought of losing Miriam and determined to do all in his power to keep her.

Reuben arrived in Nazareth sweating and tired from the journey in the sizzling hot sun. He had gone off the beaten path for shade and a rest whenever he found a grove of olive trees or an occasional bay tree. Twice he had refreshed himself at a cool stream, drinking alongside the sheep and goats. He splashed water on his face, head and feet and refreshed, continued toward his destination. He had tied the tool his father had made to his girdle, checking occasionally to assure himself it was still secure.

This being his initial trip to Nazareth, he inquired of the first person he saw as to the location of the carpenter's shop. It was but a short distance away, and his strength was revitalized as he realized that he had completed his journey.

The shop was small, smelled of freshly-cut cedar, and was kept as neat as any carpenter shop could be kept—excluding the shavings and sawdust on the floor. A man of obvious strong build was sawing a piece of wood with his back to the door, and evidently did not hear the stranger arrive. He was lithe and tan, about thirty years old, with dark brown hair and was dressed only from the waist down. His skin glistened with perspiration, and his arm and shoulder muscles stood out and rippled as he pushed and pulled the saw. As the small end of the cut piece of wood dropped to the floor, he turned to pick it up and saw Reuben from the corner of his eye.

"Peace be unto you," he said with a friendly smile, turning to face Reuben. "Is there something I can do for you?"

"I hope so. I'm looking for the carpenter named Jesus, the son of Joseph and Mary. I've brought a tool for him made by my father, David of Cana."

"I am Jesus," the strong well-modulated voice said. "Come in."

As Reuben walked in the shop and reached for the tool tied to his girdle, he was drawn by the warm, compassionate gaze of the man and could move no further. Those eyes, he thought. Never have I seen such compelling eyes. It is as if he sees right into my very soul! For a moment Reuben stood transfixed, and then he regained his composure and continued into the shop.

Meanwhile, back in Cana, Nathan chose sundown as the time of day to visit David regarding the betrothal contract. He had left Miriam sorrowful and weeping, and Esther obviously disturbed but silent. He tried to hide his own disturbance beneath a cloak of anger and indignation. He told himself that he was motivated only by a sincere love and concern for his only daughter. He merely nodded his head to his family as he left the house.

His heart was heavy, and he honestly dreaded the confrontation with his dearest friend. They had shared so much over the years, having met as boys at the synagogue school. They would recite the shema together, as well as other important Scripture. Later they sat at the feet of the rabbi and learned from him the words in the sacred scrolls. Both excelled in their oral recitations, so they were told. Each of them worked in the fields with their fathers, and David had also helped his carpenter-craftsman father—just as he himself had learned sandal-making from his own father. They had labored hard and continued to do so to this day.

Then there were the amusing times and times of adventure. In the few spare hours they had—and they were few—he and David would practice throwing spears or using slingshots. Their trips to nearby Jerusalem, required by all Hebrew males as they reached adulthood, were full of interesting experiences. He and David would often run ahead of the slower adults, teasing one another and seeing what new sights they might find on the way. In Jerusalem, they would worship together at the temple, and a spiritual bond grew between them.

In time each married a Hebrew girl of parental choice. David married Johhebed first, and they lived for awhile in his father's house until he could build one of his own. Nathan married Esther a year later but built their modest home during the year of their betrothal. The two young couples maintained a close association, and Esther and Johhebed likewise became close friends. They had not grown up together, as Johhebed came from Nazareth in Galilee. She was distantly related to David.

When their first babies were born—four years apart—they made immediate plans among themselves for a future betrothal of these two children. The dream had been realized, Nathan pondered, and now he was about to destroy that dream. No one could know his heartache, but it must be done for the sake of his beloved Mim.

He now trudged haltingly up to the gate of David's home and let himself in. He hoped David would be back from the meeting place, where they often met with

47

the other men in the village before sundown to discuss everything from news to weather and crops.

He started to knock on the door, but Johhebed opened it and was startled to see him.

"Nathan!" she exclaimed. "Come in. David just returned home from the meeting place and remarked that you were not there this evening." Then, seeing his sober and strained expression, she added, "Is something wrong? I hope no one is ill."

"No, Johhebed. No one is ill. But someone may be by the time I reach home."

"I don't understand," she replied. "Is there something we can do?"

"I need to speak with David," he said hoarsely, trying to control his emotions.

"Surely. He is up in the alliyah, reading his scrolls before our time of worship. Just go on up."

Nathan ascended the stairs to this small, private room and called to David before he presumed to pull back the curtain and enter.

"Come in, my friend," responded David, walking to the doorway to greet Nathan and embrace him.

He smiled warmly and directed his friend to a mat and sat down opposite him. David noted the strained expression on Nathan's face.

"To what do I owe the honor of this visit?" he asked, trying to begin on a friendly note. Nathan had strongly opposed him yesterday, and he hoped he had come to make amends.

"I am on a difficult mission," said Nathan, lowering his head for a moment. Then, looking up into David's questioning eyes he added in a firm voice, "I came to break the betrothal contract."

"Break the betrothal!" exclaimed the astonished David. "But, why? It has gone on for six months or more. Reuben and Miriam seem happy enough. We have drawn up plans for a house to build for them. We felt the dowry was sufficient—at least it was the best we could do. Is that it—the dowry?"

"Of course not, David!" Nathan barked. "Money has never been that important to me. You know that. In fact, I have brought the dowry with me. Not one cent has been spent. It is not the dowry. To come to the point, it is your obsession with John—John the Baptist. You know how I feel about him."

David's mouth opened in disbelief as he heard the words of his friend. "But, what on earth does that have to do with Reuben and Miriam?" he inquired in amazement. "Reuben has never gone with us to hear him nor shown any interest in the man. Why punish our children?"

"To save Miriam from God's punishment, should Reuben join you in your foolish beliefs. You know Mim would do as Reuben told her, and I will not take the chance of God's wrath falling upon her."

"I can't believe what you are saying," David said simply, in a low tone. His face was crestfallen and pale as he struggled to comprehend the development.

"You had best believe it," asserted Nathan. "I have been to our rabbi, and he is in agreement with me. He feels that this John is a rabble-rouser and a dangerous man. You and I are to meet with Rabbi Elishua tomorrow. Reuben is to come with us if he has returned. If not, he can see the rabbi later."

"You are surely losing your mind, Nathan," accused David. "Would you break your daughter's heart because of Johhebed and me?" He looked compassionately at Nathan who beheld him with an icy stare.

"She will get over it," Nathan retorted stonily. "She is young, and we will find someone for her—perhaps the son of a priest who will stick to Jewish law and tradition. God will honor us for this. Now I must leave." He rose from the mat and quickly strode toward the curtained doorway of the room. "Shalom, David. The rabbi expects us at the ninth hour tomorrow," he muttered with bowed head.

Tears were near the surface of his eyes and he quickly left before his emotions overtook him. The bond between him and David was still strong and he knew his friend was hurting. It grieved him to be the cause of this hurt, and he tried to swallow the lump that was in his throat. His mouth felt dry and his fingers trembled as he reached for the rail by the steps. Johhebed started toward him as he came down but discreetly stopped as she saw the anguish in his face. He appeared not to see her at all.

Reuben returned the following evening, full of news for the family. He was strangely warmed by his visit with his cousins and was anxious to share it all with his family and Miriam. How he had missed seeing her the previous evening, but there was still time to meet her at the well now. Would she be there? He had not been certain when he would return home so no definite plans had been made. It was about their usual meeting time now, so he decided to direct his path to the well first before going to his house—just in hopes Miriam would come.

Approaching the well, Reuben's face, which had been so full of anticipation, fell when he saw no one standing there or walking from the direction of her home. He was hot, sweaty and grimy from the journey, but he so wanted to be with her a few moments, hold her close, and kiss her sweet lips. Perhaps she will still come. But the sun was setting fast and darkness would quickly be upon the village. His hopes faded, and he turned toward his own home.

As he slowly trudged away, a small figure stood on the roof of her house and tearfully watched the young man disappear down the road.

CHAPTER FOUR

With the exception of one small oil lamp by the stairs, the house was dark as Reuben entered the doorway. The family would be up on the roof for the evening worship. Reuben rejected the impulse to rush up and see them and grabbed the lamp instead. Hastening up to his room, he removed his dusty tunic and threw it on the pallet.

He had so much to tell of the visit in Nazareth, and his heart was strangely warmed by the time spent with his cousin, Jesus. Reuben could not explain what drew him to this rugged, gentle carpenter, but he had an urgency inside to see him again and listen to the words he imparted.

Mary likewise impressed him with her sweet, loving spirit and kindness to him. Two brothers were present also, but they had little to say and noticeably stayed out of any conversation with Jesus, scoffing and grimacing at their older brother as he spoke.

Reuben pondered these things as he poured water into a washbasin from the pitcher his mother always kept filled. He was reminded of her constant goodness to him and his heart filled with gratitude. Dousing the refreshing liquid over his face, head, arms and chest, and dipping his feet one at a time in the bowl to remove the heavy dust, he yearned for the coolness of the springs he had encountered on his journey.

Dressed in a clean tunic and a change of sandals, he mounted the outside stairway to the roof. No one spoke as he padded softly to a cushion and let his agile body down with the ease of well-conditioned youth. David glanced warmly and nodded at his son in greeting, but kept on reading the scroll. Johhebed and Rhoda smiled briefly, quickly returning their gazes to David as he rocked back and forth and read the words of Isaiah concerning the coming of the Messiah.

Reuben found it difficult to concentrate on the words his father was reading. His heart had become heavy because he did not see Miriam as expected. He had returned to Cana singing—in the same manner as he had left town—fully expecting to see his beloved waiting for him. When she was not there, he felt disturbed. Was she ill? Had there been an accident? He hoped his family could enlighten him. The families were close and news always traveled quickly in the small village.

Glancing over at his mother, he noticed a sadness in her face. What had happened to make her look like that? He could not discern anything revealing from his father's expression, for David always read the holy Scriptures with a certain melancholy, deeply moved by the plight of the Jews (due mainly to their own disobedience to God) over the centuries.

David's voice rose as he read the prophetic Scriptures, and soon the family bowed in prayer as the resonant tones sent up petitions.

The prayer over, Reuben quickly jumped up to embrace his family. His father's strong grip on his arm indicated he was to stay and talk. He looked to his mother and was startled to see her cheeks stained with tears as she and Rhoda softly and quickly headed for the stairs. They did not utter a word, and Reuben knew something was amiss. It had to concern Miriam! Why won't they come out and tell me instead of behaving as if someone had...oh, no! he thought as a hard lump constricted his throat and his face blanched. Miriam couldn't be...

Turning to his father, he impatiently watched the older man carefully roll up the sacred scroll with bowed head and somber expression. Reuben knew better than to hurry any conversation. If there were news he would be told in his father's own timing. That was David's way. The young man recalled that as a child of ten he waited two full days to be told that Asa the family donkey had slipped on a stone and fallen off a low cliff outside Jerusalem, landing head first on a pile of rocks to his demise. When David had returned home without the beloved ass, the children assumed he had strayed and gotten lost, until they were told later of the accident by a tearful father. David had a soft heart concerning the helpless.

Now the waiting was interminable, and Reuben's heart began to pound in dread anticipation. At last the scroll was put away in a cedar box, and David indicated two cushions for them to sit upon. He bowed his head for a moment and then looked with compassion upon Reuben before he spoke.

"Nathan has broken the betrothal, my son. And it is all because of your mother and me. I'm so sorry...so very sorry!" His voice cracked as he spoke, and he laid his hand upon the young man's shoulder as if to support him.

"The betrothal broken!" gasped Reuben in complete disbelief. "But, why, Father? And why because of you and Mother? I don't understand! And what about Miriam? She is...all right?" he added in a quivering voice.

"Yes, my son, to your last question. We know nothing concerning Miriam's feelings, of course, but Nathan and I went to see the rabbi, and Nathan nullified the contract."

Feeling a certain relief that Miriam was at least alive, Reuben sighed deeply and continued his questioning. "But you still haven't told me why, Father. What could you and Mother possibly have done?" Then he remembered what Miriam had told him before he left for Nazareth. He remembered her anxious concern about her father's words to her mother. He himself had planned to visit Nathan to straighten things out, but in his heart he had not taken the threat seriously.

"It is because we follow the teachings of the Baptist," answered David sadly. "I could not convince him that you and Miriam had no interest in John and should not be punished because of us. But he would not listen."

Reuben became withdrawn and silent. It was almost as if he had been turned to stone. A mixture of thoughts ran through his mind, and his emotions began to churn and burn his very being. His anguish knew no bounds at the thought of losing his beloved

Miriam. Small wonder she was not at the well. At least she is all right. He was filled with gratitude for that—gratitude which blended into pity for the beloved girl who so obviously loved him as he loved her.

How was she taking this terrible turn of events? Is she right now shedding tears in the privacy of her room? How could her father do this to her? Did he have to hurt Miriam because of his preconceived notions about the Baptizer—without even hearing him? Does he think that just because my parents found John interesting it would affect Miriam and me? How very foolish and stiff-necked that assumption was!

Anger began to take the place of anguish, and Reuben's fists tightened as his hardened eyes met those of his father's compassionate ones.

"Why did you let this happen?" he barked in a rare outburst at David. He felt his face reddening and his jaw and facial muscles tighten. "Why have you made so much of that man in front of Nathan, especially after he came to see you and told you how he felt? Why couldn't you have kept silent?"

"I could not keep silent, my son," answered David in an even voice filled with conviction. "God knows my heart, and it would be folly for me to lead Nathan to believe I might change my mind. And I would advise you to hold your temper with me," he added, his black eyes smoldering and holding Reuben's with a sudden steely gaze.

"I'm sorry, Father," Reuben apologized with downcast eyes. Looking once more at his father he ventured, "But can you blame me for my anger and resentment? This will change my whole life...and destroy my dreams!"

"We are all beset with problems to vex us," David answered, running his fingers through his thick black hair. Bracing himself with his hands on the cushion, he leaned back and added, "Perhaps you yourself should go and speak with Nathan. You have nothing to lose. But I urge you to speak with all respect. Hostility will only bring you disfavor in his eyes."

A sudden brightness and urgency changed Reuben's expression into one of hope: hope that is a driving force of life, without which survival is futile. There is still hope, he reasoned. Isn't that what I had originally planned to do anyway—talk with Nathan?

"I'll do it!" he exclaimed suddenly, jumping up from his cushion. "I'll see him tomorrow at the first opportunity. Surely I can convince him that Miriam and I have no interest in the man named John. I can even promise..."

"Make no promise you cannot keep," said the father wisely in a firm voice, as he stroked his curly black beard.

"But Father, I have no intention of even seeing or hearing the man in the wilderness."

"I had not intention either, until your mother and I traveled in that vicinity. Curiosity alone finally drew us to listen to him. Now we feel God led us there." David slowly raised up from his cushion, pushing himself with one hand flat on the floor of the rooftop. "Let us try and sleep now. Go quietly so as not to awaken your mother."

"Shalom, Father. May you sleep well," Reuben whispered as he followed the older man down the stairs.

Turning into his own cubicle, Reuben pondered the new turn of events with apprehension. A slim ray of hope dulled the cutting blade of despair. He threw himself down on his pallet with the rash impulsiveness of youth and lay on his back in the darkness, silently cursing the man named John. So what if he was a relative! He had never seen him.

"If Nathan refuses to change his mind," he whispered softly through clenched teeth, bending his fingers into tight fists, "I won't know who to be angrier at...Nathan or my own parents! Oh, God" he petitioned, "please help me! Help us!"

Rolling over on his side and gazing out the small window at the stars winking in the blackness of the night, Reuben further gave vent to his feelings by pounding on the edge of his pallet. "Are you there, God? Do you hear me? Why are you letting this thing happen to Miriam and me?"

Miriam lay on her own pallet trying to swallow the lump in her throat. Tears continued to drop on her pillow as she relived her father's pronouncement of the night before.

She should really not be surprised, she considered. Nathan was a strong-willed man, completely devout in his faith, and he followed God's word to the letter. If a new way was not written in the Scriptures he would have nothing to do with it. She could not fault him for this, but could he not understand that his training had also rubbed off on her? She wanted no changes herself and felt secure in their way of life. The prayers of her father had always stirred her. She had loved helping her mother keep his black robe, his prayer shawl and his sandals clean and free from dust. Why did he not trust her?

"I wish I had never been betrothed!" she cried softly to herself. "Now I shall never marry, for there could be no one but Reuben in my life. Why is Papa so unreasonable? The Baptist means nothing to Reuben and me!"

"Reuben," she whispered, her mood changing from anger to compassion and devotion. "I saw you come almost to the well this evening and then turn back. You walked so vigorously on your way into town. You stopped short when you saw the well. Then you slowly turned and walked toward your house with your head bowed. What were you thinking, Reuben?" she mused sadly. "Did you feel I had forgotten to meet you—or did you possibly worry?"

Miriam tossed fitfully, unable to fall asleep and full of imaginings and sorrow. Was this all a dream or was it really happening? "Oh, dear God, please let it all be a dream."

Sleep finally overcame her, thrusting her into nightmares which caused her to cry out and her heart to pound wildly as she awoke in a cold sweat. Her mother ran to her each time, returning to her own pallet after being reassured that her daughter was only dreaming. Esther sought solace from Nathan, who enveloped her in his strong arms and held her close until sleep came to his precious wife. Sleep was a stranger for him that night, as he felt his daughter's sorrow.

Johhebed arose sooner than usual the following morning. Sleep had eluded her also, and the dark shadows under her eyes were telltale evidence. Her heart was heavy under the cloud of despair which rested over the household. She tried to find reassurance in the fact that Reuben planned to visit Nathan. David had shared this with her before he had dropped off to sleep the previous evening.

But she had known Nathan for a long period of time. He rarely gave in to something he had set his mind against. He was typical of the stubborn breed of men the Scriptures so often mentioned. Change had no part in his life. He would not listen to Reuben, she reflected.

Tiptoeing downstairs, she slipped out into the courtyard for a moment's meditation. The cool of early morning was refreshing to her sluggish body, and she put her head back and breathed in the air which smelled of lilies and early morning fires. A brown lizard ran up the courtyard wall and stopped to warily survey the area for danger. A turtledove cooed for its mate, then all was silent. Moments like these were precious to Johhebed and restored her soul.

"You're up early, aren't you Mother?" spoke a familiar voice. Startled, she jumped and turned to see Reuben behind her. He placed his hands on her shoulders and looked her solemnly in the eyes. "Do not set food out for me this morning. I could not swallow a bite. Did you not sleep well?" he asked, looking at her drawn countenance.

"No, my son," answered Johhebed truthfully. "I am heavy hearted over your broken betrothal. Your father and I feel so responsible, and yet...we would never mean you harm, nor can we turn back on our convictions. We pray Nathan will listen to you."

"He must!" retorted Reuben sharply. "He is a cruel man if he doesn't."

"Nathan is not cruel—stubborn, perhaps. Things will turn out well, Reuben," she said, with love for her son giving her tired face a glow. "Now tell me about your visit to Nazareth. How did you find Mary? It has been some years since I have seen her."

"Mary was well and anxious for news of you," Reuben replied. Then walking over to the courtyard wall and leaning sideways against it, he paused a moment before turning his head toward Johhebed and looking past her with a far-off expression. "This cousin of mine—Jesus—he is different from the rest of the family."

"What do you mean different?" questioned Johhebed.

"It's hard to say," answered Reuben, knitting his eyebrows together in a frown. "He's pleasant enough… warm, outgoing, friendly…but it's more than that. It's like he sees inside of you…knows your mind when you speak with him. I felt very drawn to him. I invited them to the wedding as you asked. Mary and Jesus both said they would be there. Mary is planning to help you with the wedding feast. Now there will be no wedding."

"Don't give up entirely, Reuben. You said you were going to see Nathan. He rises early, so you won't have to wait long."

"I'll leave right after morning prayers," Reuben replied. "I'd like to be at his shop before others come in. Our town gossip, Simon, spends much time there and would love such a tidbit to pass around. Remember how quickly he spread the word about Amos losing the hind part of his tunic to a goat?"

The recollection brought a laugh from both of them and eased the tension which had already begun to build. Johhebed patted Reuben's arm and proceeded with the business of making up the bread for the morning meal. She had lit a fire when she first came downstairs, so the stones would be hot by now.

When David came down later, he kissed his wife and went straight to his place in the dining room, standing quietly in meditation after greeting Reuben. Johhebed had put out the fire, removed the ashes, and placed thin layers of dough on the stones lining the earth oven. The smell of baking bread was tempting to the appetite, but Reuben still had no desire to eat. The tense knot was still in his stomach, and he only hoped he would not heave.

Soon David threw back his head and with closed eyes thanked God for the new day and asked for protection and health for his family. He paused a moment and added a prayer for wisdom for his son.

As Johhebed and Rhoda brought in fruit and the hot bread, David looked at his son anxiously. It grieved him to know that Reuben was hurting—unnecessarily so, he felt—because of the impulsive act of his best friend, Nathan. Nathan had always been stubborn, he reflected, but his many good points far outweighed this negative one. His devoutness was the root cause of this rash act, David knew, so he could not feel too harshly toward him. But his heart reached out to Reuben and Miriam.

"Do you still plan to talk with Nathan?" he asked his son.

"Yes, Father," Reuben answered soberly. "I am leaving right now."

"Before you eat?" This was surprising to David for it was usually difficult to satisfy the growing young man at mealtimes. He often wondered if the boy had hollow legs!

"I want no food now. I can eat later."

"Go in peace then and remember the words of King Solomon, 'A soft answer turns away wrath.' I urge you to hold your tongue and use it discreetly."

"I'll try, Father, but you know how hot-headed Nathan gets. Wish me well. My future happiness is at stake."

Reuben turned and strode out of the house quickly, trying to suppress the anxiety and heaviness which suffused him like an unwelcome intruder. His palms were moist and clammy and he felt his stomach churning. A foreboding shattered the hope he had upon arising. He knew he must do his utmost to try and convince Nathan to reverse his decision.

A group of women was at the well as he walked along the dusty road, and he wondered if one was Miriam. Their backs were turned, and they clustered together so he could not discern identities at a distance. How he ached to see her and hold her close…to feel the softness of her lips responding to his own. I must succeed this morning! I must! A new courage arose in him, and he strode faster down the street which led to the sandal-making shop.

Nathan had already arrived and was seated at his bench replacing a sole on a well-worn sandal. He was intent on his work and sang a hallel as he skillfully attached the thick leather to the inner sole and sandal straps. Reuben breathed deeply and wiped his palms on his tunic before entering. He was glad Nathan was alone.

"Shalom, Nathan," he greeted his beloved's father. "May I speak with you a few moments?"

Nathan turned around on his workbench and paled a bit as he saw Reuben. "Why, yes, Reuben. Sit over here by me," he said, indicating a crude wooden stool. "I have been expecting you sometime today, though not quite this soon. How was your journey to Nazareth?" he asked, avoiding Reuben's direct look by brushing some small scraps of hide onto the floor.

"I fared well, thank you. Good weather followed me, and I spent a pleasant time with my cousins. But can we discuss the subject for which I came? I cannot understand the thing which has taken place—the breaking of our betrothal. Why, Nathan, why?"

"Did not David tell you why? I was sure that he would," answered Nathan, busying himself with the sandal as he talked.

"He told me that it was because he and my mother had begun to follow the teachings of John—the Baptist, as they call him. But surely you know that Miriam and I have no intention of following him. What does that have to do with us?"

Nathan put down the sandal and thundered, "It has everything to do with Miriam! If she married you and you found merit in the teachings your parents follow, God will surely judge her—as he no doubt will your parents and you! No, Reuben, such a union cannot be. Life is hard enough being under the domination of Rome and often wondering where the tax money will come from. Another worry is too much. I did the only thing I could do."

"What of Miriam? How does she feel about this?" questioned Reuben, as he fought to restrain his temper in the presence of the older man.

"She is unhappy. But she will get over it, as you will also. You are both young and have much life ahead of you. You will make a good match, and Miriam will not stay single. You will always be like a son to us, Reuben...but a son-in-law, no. I'm sorry, but that's the way it is. Now I must get to work. Please excuse me."

"But sir, can't we discuss this more? Miriam and I have no intention..."

"Enough, Reuben!" Nathan interrupted harshly. "I have no more time to talk about this now. Besides, it is settled. I suggest you see the rabbi and tell him that you have talked with me. Shalom." And he turned to his work, dismissing Reuben with a wave of his hand. The talk was over. So final. So like Nathan.

Later that very day a message was sent to Mary of Nazareth by way of a small caravan passing through.

CHAPTER FIVE

Jonas returned to Cana from Judea with much news for the interested villagers. He had delivered the piece of embroidery to Miriam's friend, Rebecca, and brought back a tiny alabaster jar of perfume from her for Miriam's wedding gift.

"She sends word she will try to come for the wedding if it is at a time she is not needed in the fields," he told Miriam.

"There will be no wedding, Jonas," she informed him sadly, with a touch of coldness, trying to repress the tears which threatened to surface. "The betrothal is broken." She fingered the beautiful alabaster jar thoughtfully.

"Broken!" Jonas exclaimed, his eyes narrowing. "But, why? This has been your family's plan for many years. How could this be?"

"It is Papa's desire. I cannot talk about it," she choked. "I'm sure he means well," she added, not wishing to cast aspersions upon her father.

"I'm sorry, little friend," the older man answered gently. "I'll ask no more about it. Shalom for now." He discreetly turned and strode out of the courtyard and down the road before Esther came down from the roof, where she had been checking the clothes laid out to dry.

Miriam was silent when her mother entered the courtyard, and Esther deemed it best to leave her alone with her thoughts. She had tried endlessly over the past few weeks to bring her daughter into cheerful conversation, but she knew the hurt she was suffering and turned much to prayer instead.

Jonas joined the men that evening in the village and was besieged with questions about the state of affairs in and around Jerusalem, as well as what caravans he had met and what other things of interest he encountered. Outside news was always a welcome diversion to the villagers.

"What did you hear about Tiberius?" asked Nathan. "And how about the Roman soldiers? Are they as cruel and arrogant as ever? Only today two rode through here acting pompous and raucous, obviously asking for trouble."

"The Roman soldiers are the same," answered Jonas. "People in Jerusalem cower with fear each time they hear hoofbeats coming down the road. And sometimes rightly so. One day I saw one of the mounted guards spit at an old man who could not cross the road fast enough to suit him. It was all I could do to hold my tongue.

"As for Tiberius, there is still talk about his bust being paraded in the streets by the Roman soldiers. This is a sore spot with our people. They cannot forget the revulsion it caused them when it was brought through the streets on the Day of Atonement. They call it idolatry, and rightly so."

"Did you get to Joppa?" asked a young man named Nathanael. "I hear the trading there is corrupt."

"Yes, I went just out of curiosity and to add to my purse. Help is sometimes needed on the piers, and I'm still strong. Payment is not good, as the big cargoes land at Tyre and Sidon. There is always corruption where material things are concerned.

"There was one event of interest. A border incident occurred near Caesarea between Roman soldiers and some hot-headed Jews protesting the tax. But the skirmish was soon put down—thanks to Augustus's Pax Romana, as it is called. That was one thing in favor of Augustus, I would say. We even had hopes for his stepson, Tiberius, but word comes to us that he is a spoiled pleasure seeker. I predict our taxes will go even higher."

"And what about John the Baptist? Did you see or hear him?" inquired David eagerly. The hum of conversation subsided at the question, and the place became silent. Nathan and a few others glowered at David, but David kept his eyes riveted upon Jonas.

"Yes," replied Jonas, "I saw him twice—once on my way and again on my return. I stayed two days on my way back."

"You wasted three days on that rabble-rousing bit of humanity?" thundered Nathan venomously. "That's an affront to your own intelligence, Jonas! But then you know how I feel. I'm sorry to say that about Johhebed's cousin," he added, looking over at David, who merely glanced at him soberly.

"Yes, Nathan, I do know how you feel," answered Jonas. "But if you could just listen to the man. He shows us sins we've been unconscious of. He says the kingdom of heaven is at hand and that Messiah will come soon. And he teaches true repentance. What is so wrong with all that?"

"But the baptism," Nathan retorted, ignoring the question, "that is not in Jewish law. Does he substitute that for God's law requiring animal sacrifice? And he is not even a member of the priesthood. Who is he to talk of repentance? No, Jonas, he is surely out of God's will. Only Elijah will usher in Messiah. Does not Scripture tell us that?"

Some even say that John is Elijah. But let us not argue, Nathan. Life is too short—and so is your temper," Jonas added with a chuckle. "Only time will tell about the Baptizer. Meanwhile, have a look at my sandals. The rocky roads I have been on have chewed them up…to say nothing about the bottom of my feet. I hope you are well supplied with camel hide."

"I have a little, but I'll have to trade for some soon."

"Why not get some down by the Jordan, Nathan?" asked Aaron laughingly, making reference to John's territory.

"That's enough!" reprimanded David. "Let's leave that matter alone. It's almost sundown, friends, and time for evening worship. Shalom and sleep well."

The group dispersed to their respective homes, and David considered the news and remarks of Jonas. He regretted Nathan's outburst and noticed that the temper of the group was mainly with him. If only they could all hear the man, he yearned.

David also harbored the embryo of a new idea as he plodded homeward up the natural slope of the land. His son's future was much on his mind, and he was anxious that Reuben marry and start his own family. The youth was learning the trade of a craftsman very well and would one day take over the family business. A new interest should take his mind off of Miriam. Reuben was not stubborn, but he was terribly depressed and angry. David could not condemn him for that.

In the privacy of their own room that evening, David and Johhebed whispered their hopes and dreams to each other. They had only been in Cana two years, and most of the marriageable young women there were already betrothed. Whom could they consider as a possible mate for their only son? they pondered.

"How about Deborah, your niece in Capernaum?" Johhebed volunteered. "The one whose betrothed was killed by soldiers on the road to Jerusalem last year? You know, David, it seems only like yesterday that terrible thing happened."

"It was actually just before Passover," David answered. "The family were on the way to Jerusalem and Roman soldiers rode by and mocked them, calling them 'Jewish scum.' Caleb's temper flared and he jumped off the cart, lashing out with his fists at the legs of the offending officers." David stopped, his voice choking up in remembrance.

"How awful it was that the family stood helpless as they watched one of the soldiers cut off his hands with a sword, while the other one held them back as Caleb lay screaming and bleeding to death. When the guards finally left, it was too late to save the poor boy. It was monstrous!"

"Let's not think of it, my dear wife. It's much too upsetting." He held her close for a few moments before continuing. "Deborah has never married, has she?

Perhaps you have a possible solution for Reuben," he considered.

"She is a beautiful girl," Johhebed said softly.

"Perhaps it's time we paid the family a visit—you and I and Rhoda. Reuben can keep the shop," suggested David.

"Yes, that sounds wise," answered his wife with a smile.

The idea continued to germinate and take root in the minds of the parents of Reuben, and the departure date was finally set.

Nothing explicit was said to Reuben as David and Johhebed prepared for the fairly short journey. They merely indicated they had a desire to see the family and would combine business with pleasure. In their wisdom, they realized their plan would be met with intense opposition until Reuben himself would discover Deborah as a lovely and desirable person. He was still too full of resentment for them to suggest any such proposal at present. Reuben suspected nothing of their plans as they left Cana in their cart.

Reuben himself was desperate to see Miriam. She had confined her outside activities to morning visits to the well with the other village women and girls, and he had no way to contact her. She was always surrounded by others.

Finally, the long-awaited opportunity arose. After his parents had left on their journey, Miriam's brother, Jacob, came by the wood-carving shop with a message from Miriam. The lad had been sworn to secrecy by his sister, with the threat of informing their parents about a recent misdemeanor if he told them of this visit to Reuben. Miriam had caught Jacob tasting heavily of his father's wine late one evening. The effect was to make him drunken to the point of going up to the roof and imitating his father reading the sacred scrolls, rocking back and forth unsteadily and giggling like a fool. Miriam had heard him from her room and had taken a bowl of water she had bathed in (and was saving for her mother's plants in the morning) and sloshed it in his face. As he stood dripping wet and staring incredulously at his sister, she eyed him with a sardonic expression, as if daring him to complain.

The effects of the unpleasant dousing were sobering. Miriam deemed her present bit of blackmail quite appropriate. The thoroughly ashamed Jacob was only too willing to oblige.

"Miriam has a message for you," the boy said timidly to Reuben, slipping quietly into the shop after looking around in all directions lest his father see him.

"Come in, come in," begged Reuben, smiling and wiping his hands on his stained apron. "Please give me any word you can on Miriam!"

"She...well...she wants to see you," said the nervous young man.

"And I want to see her! But how...when...where?"

"She said to tell you she has to take some broth to old Zipporah, who is ill, at the sixth hour. There's a garden in back of the house which has a grove of trees. She will meet you in the grove."

"Nothing can stop me from going, Jacob! Thank you for bringing me this news! I'm grateful." He patted the boy on the shoulder. "Now be off," he added, "lest someone comes by. Your secret is safe with me."

The boy slipped out quietly and brushed the telltale sawdust off his feet and sandals. He had completed his errand successfully. Now his misdemeanor was safe with Miriam. The score was even.

Just before the sixth hour, a middle-aged stranger came into the shop to describe a small chest he wanted made of oak. Since it was to contain carving on the top, Reuben tried to tell the man, who lived in neighboring Garis, that it would be best that he wait until David returned home, inasmuch as he was the one who did the carving. The man was insistent that Reuben could take the directions. Furthermore, he would not be able to stay over in Cana. He gave a long description of the journey he was taking—much to the distress of Reuben who was agitated that his plans to meet Miriam were being interrupted. He knew he must listen patiently to the stranger, for his father would make a good sum on the sale. He hoped that his inner irritation would not show.

"We have no oak at the present," informed Reuben, "but we can begin the chest as soon as we obtain some. But about the carving, would you simply leave that to my father's discretion? He has a good reputation along those lines. I do none of it myself."

"I have heard of your father's reputation, young man, and that is why I am here now. I shall trust him. The chest is to be a wedding gift for my niece. I can pick it up in two months when I return through Cana. My name is Jahdai. Here are two denari to help with your purchase of the wood. Shalom.

The man turned and left.

The hour was already late, and Reuben felt certain he would miss Miriam altogether. Why did this have to happen? he questioned with exasperation. He took off his stained apron, brushed the sawdust out of his hair, and off his sandals and feet, wiped his face with a towel, and hurriedly left the shop in the direction of the home of the elderly widow, Zipporah. She lived on the outskirts of the village in a rundown house of clay.

Reuben all but ran, hoping against hope that he would not be too late to see Miriam. What would she think about his tardiness? Would she understand and wait for him? These thoughts ran through his mind as he raced to his destination. The street was empty when he came in sight of the house, and his heart began to pound in anticipation and dread at the same time. He anticipated seeing his beloved as if she were still there, but he dreaded the thought of having missed her because of long-winded Jahdai. He would soon know.

Skirting the house itself and not wanting to disturb Zipporah, Reuben went straight to the grove of fig trees in the rear of the house. He saw no one there, and his heart immediately sank. He was too late after all. He could not blame Miriam, for she could not stay away from home too long herself. With the one fragment of hope remaining in him he softly whispered, "Miriam."

"Yes, Reuben," answered the sweet voice he loved so dearly. Then a laughing head poked around the low branches of a tree beside the back of the house and the two lovers ran to each other with arms outstretched.

"Oh, my love," groaned Reuben in the ecstasy of holding Miriam in his arms again. "How I have missed you and wished for this moment!" He undid her braids and ran his fingers through her thick black hair, kissing her lips with a tender passion such as he had never done before

"Reuben," Miriam moaned, as she responded to his kiss, blending her lips to his searching ones and encircling his waist with her arms. All too soon the moment was over for them, and they knew they must talk quickly.

"Reuben, I'm desolate at what Papa did! What are we to do?" she asked, restoring her hair into braids for the sake of discretion.

"We bide our time right now, but you know that I love you and still want to make you my wife."

"Yes, I do know that. And I feel the same about you, Reuben. Papa says I will marry someone else sometime, but I cannot do that. You are the one I love, and I will have no other."

Reuben again encircled her in his arms and kissed the top of her head, her eyes, and her cheeks, finally softly and briefly kissing her red lips once more.

"When can we meet again?" he asked anxiously. "I cannot go on without seeing you."

"Nor I, Reuben. Zipporah needs my help right now, and I told her I would come after my work is finished in the morning. How can I get word to you? Papa will be working in the vineyard, he said. I heard him ask Jacob to go down to the shop and sweep and clean up. He could get word to you if I go by there on my way here. But what about your father? Will he not be at your shop?"

"Not tomorrow. He and my mother are in Capernaum and should not be home until the following day. Oh, our God will surely work things out for us, Miriam. I don't believe he wants us separated like this."

"Nor, I, Reuben. Now I must make haste to return home. Until tomorrow then, my love."

They kissed briefly, and Miriam ran out to the road and took the direction of her home. Reuben discreetly waited a few moments and took the other direction in a roundabout way to his shop. A song was in his heart, bursting to come out, but he kept his silence lest someone wonder why he would be so happy this soon after a broken betrothal. He would have to watch himself.

Miriam was flushed as she hurriedly entered her courtyard, and Esther noticed that the usual sadness was not present in her face. A suspicion began to seep into the mother's mind, but she did not wish to express it openly as yet.

"How was Zipporah?" she asked her daughter.

"Quite weak, Mama, but she seemed to enjoy the broth. She needs help tomorrow, and I told her I would come after I finished my chores around here. Will that be all right?"

"Of course, my dear. We need to help her all we can. Perhaps I can go with you."

Disturbed at the very thought of her mother accompanying her, thus negating her plans to see Reuben again, Miriam quickly said, "Oh, that won't be necessary, Mama. All I need to do is warm up the rest of the broth and perhaps take her some fruit and bread. I can bring her soiled clothing home to wash here and take back sometime tomorrow. I can easily do that myself."

Esther noticed that the girl averted her eyes and showed a slight reddening of the face, but she decided to pursue the matter no further. Something has happened, of that she was certain. Miriam had been in such a deep depression since her betrothal was broken, and she was hurting in other ways also.

"What will others say of me?" she had asked her mother one day in discussing the situation. "I feel so ashamed...as if I had done something wrong myself.

My friends are asking questions when we meet at the well in the mornings, and you know I cannot denounce Papa. Whatever can I say to them? They are most inquisitive, and some even laugh about it, saying that Reuben will no doubt find another quickly."

"You can simply tell them that it was a family matter, which is very true. You need say no more, though we are not ashamed of your father's convictions. Many would simply not understand his devoutness to God and might gossip about him. We surely don't want that.

"As for Reuben finding someone else, you had better make up your mind to that, my daughter. David and Johhebed will want him to marry and start a family, so don't be surprised if this should happen. It will be difficult for you at first, but of course our hopes are that you will also marry."

"Never!" Miriam cried out. "I cannot give myself to someone else when I love Reuben!"

Tears began to run down her cheeks, and she quickly busied herself with the weaving she had started.

They had not spoken of the matter recently, and Miriam had become withdrawn and unapproachable. Now the radiant expression on her face bemused Esther. She discerned that it had to have something to do with Reuben. Nothing else would give her eyes a new sparkle and a smile to her lips. Even Nathan noticed the change in her that evening and asked his wife for an explanation.

"I don't know what has happened to her," Esther replied cautiously. "Perhaps her depression is simply wearing off, and she found it pleasant to go somewhere other than the well. She took some broth to Zipporah today, as the dear soul is ill with a fever and aching bones. I'm sure that must account for Miriam's change in attitude. I know of no other reason."

"I only hope she didn't meet up with Reuben," said Nathan, his eyes narrowing. I have warned her to stay away from him."

"Esther's pulse quickened, for she had the same suspicion and was hopeful of protecting her daughter from a scene with her father. The girl had gone through enough lately. Perhaps it was time to take some positive steps in her behalf.

"Isn't it time now to think about another alliance for her?" she asked gently, hoping to divert Nathan from the matter at hand.

"Absolutely," agreed Nathan. "But who can we find for her in Cana? I've given the matter some serious thought and cannot come up with a single young man I would want Mim to marry. There is Nathanael, but again there is a complication. He says his very close friend, Philip of Bethsaida, has been going to hear John the Baptist. Nathanael himself rather laughs at the idea, but then again, Philip is very close to him and could be a real influence.

"Then there is Phinehas, the son of our rabbi, but he is leaving to study under Gamaliel, the teacher and member of the Sanhedrin, and wants no part of marriage right now. Frankly, I can't think of anyone around here. We may have to make an alliance with someone elsewhere. But where, I do not know."

"Surely there will be someone," said Esther assuredly. "Miriam would make a good wife, and I look forward to many grandchildren."

"And I also," Nathan affirmed. "But now it is time for evening worship, and we must ascend to the roof."

The following morning, Miriam excitedly performed her routine tasks and made absolutely certain that her father was working in the large vineyard in back of the house. Jacob had been sent to the shop right after the morning meal, so things were going as planned. She braided her hair, since it was the customary sign of an unmarried maiden. She wished she could let it hang loose for Reuben. Placing some grapes and a loaf of bread in a small basket to take to Zipporah, Miriam kissed her mother good-bye and headed down the road in the direction of Zipporah's house.

She knew she must go first to her father's shop, but that was only slightly out of her way. No one could see her from her house. The thought entered her mind that her father might decide to walk over to the shop for something, but she dismissed it as being very unlikely.

Jacob was brushing off the workbench when she got there, and she knew she must accomplish her mission in haste.

"Run quickly and tell Reuben I am on my way to Zipporah's now," she said. "Please don't tarry in any way. Papa could decide to come over here, you know. Hurry! Run!"

"Oh, all right," said Jacob sullenly, "but this is the last time I'll do it!" and he bolted down the road.

Miriam hastened to Zipporah's and found her elderly friend lying down but smiling. Her face was pale, but her eyes glistened warmly as she looked at Miriam.

"You are a sweet child," she said weakly. "What would I do without you?" She grasped Miriam's hand with her own trembling one, squeezing her fingers gently.

"Oh, someone else would come," Miriam said cheerily. "I've brought you some fruit and bread if you feel like eating. I'll light a fire for you anyway and give you some more of the broth I brought yesterday. You must have some of that. And please tell me where your soiled linens and things are so I can take them home and wash them. I can do it when we are washing ours."

"May God bless you for your kindness, child. The soiled things are all in a pile over in the corner. One of my neighbors gathered them for me last evening. If they don't dry in time before the Sabbath, don't fret about it. I won't need them until the day following."

Miriam lit the fire outside. While the stones were getting hot she swept out the shabby, dark room which was Zipporah's living quarters. The place depressed her—so dark and nothing to brighten it. She poured some water from a pitcher which the same thoughtful neighbor had brought, bathed Zipporah with a cloth, and washed up a bowl and cup from the previous day. All the time, she watched out of the corner of her eye for the arrival of Reuben.

Just as she was giving Zipporah the warmed up broth she saw the familiar figure coming down the road. Her heart leaped with joy, but she knew she must complete all of her tasks first before going out to the grove to greet him. He knew to wait for her. Oh, what joy it was to know that she would see and touch him again!

"Are you sure there is nothing else I can do for you, Zipporah?" inquired Miriam, leaning down to kiss the kindly woman on the brow after she completed her tasks.

"No, dear one. You have done more than enough already. Thank you, and may God's blessings be upon you."

"Picking up the soiled clothes and linens and tying them into a bundle, Miriam started toward the doorway, turned and smiled and said, "I'll check on you tomorrow, Zipporah. Shalom." And she left.

Her feet carried her swiftly around the back to the grove of trees. This time Reuben was sitting at the foot of a tree waiting for her. He jumped up quickly when he saw her coming and ran to embrace her. The place was thick with foliage and was private, so the couple had no inhibitions about being seen.

"Oh, my love," said Reuben softly in her ear. "How long can we go on like this? It will soon be difficult to even meet." He kissed her brow as he talked.

"I know, Reuben. Your family will be back by tomorrow, and I fear Jacob will not take to being my messenger any longer. He said so today. Besides, Papa would not let him leave the shop, and you could not leave yours. Now that Jonas is back, Papa will not be spending time in the vineyard either. But, surely, we will think of something. Right now I want you to hold me," she murmured.

Miriam was almost frightened at her physical awareness of Reuben now as compared to several weeks ago. He was the first and only man to kiss her outside of immediate family members, who usually gave her a peck on the cheek. The first shy kiss from Reuben awakened her desire for more, and now she found herself responding in a way she never dreamed was possible. A passionate stirring within her made her wonder where it would lead, but she knew she would remain pure and felt sure of Reuben's respect.

Her mother had told her little about physical relationships between men and women, but she learned from talk at the well that some things were beyond decorum. She understood little that was said, but she was able to put a few things together from idle remarks, the laughter that ensued, and an occasional descriptive account by one of the more flagrant young women in the village. She suspected two of them as being immoral, but she had no proof of this. When she would ask Esther about it, she was told not to gossip—even with her.

Now she put her arms around Reuben's waist and felt his rippling muscles as he embraced her and placed his lips on hers in a tender but desirous fashion. Every moment was precious with them and neither wanted to break away. Reuben again loosened her braids and ran his callused hands through her luxuriant hair and across the back of her neck, sending tingling sensations through her body.

"Oh, my sweet," he whispered, " I know we must part now, but I want to drink in all I can of you. We don't know when we can meet again like this, and I want to remember every second of our time together."

He lifted his head and put his hands on her shoulders, holding her gaze for awhile. He dropped his hands as she braided her hair and secured the ends with the pieces of loose hair he had slipped off of them. She knew she must leave, and tears welled close to the surface of her eyes.

"When?"...she muttered and could say no more.

"We will find a way, my love. We both must go now. Try not to fret. Just remember that I love you and will be thinking of you constantly."

"And I you, Reuben. Shalom for now. I love you too."

Miriam turned, picked up her bundle and slipped quietly around the house and down the road. Reuben, deeply stirred, waited a few moments and retraced the same route to the shop he had used the day before. Something must be worked out for them. He did not like the idea of deceiving their parents and meeting on the sly. But he had to see her. She was his whole world.

David and Johhebed returned home around noon the following day, weary but encouraged by the journey. The weariness came from the extreme heat of the morning as they traveled, along with the jostling around in the cart as the donkeys, Saul and Samson, paid no heed to the smoother parts of the road.

After leaving Johhebed at the house, David went straight to the shop. He was anxious to see his son and get to his work. He had met a caravan in Capernaum which carried—among other things—a few small but choice pieces of cedar which he could always use. The bargaining with the crafty Arab was difficult, but a fair price was eventually reached. Now he would unload it and put it to good use.

"Greetings, Reuben!" he called out as he stepped into the shop, carrying a portion of his load of wood. "How have things gone in my absence?"

"Greetings, Father!" Reuben rejoined as he dropped the plumb line he was using to check the straightness of a board. "Everything is going well here at the shop. I have an order for a small carved chest to be completed in two months. I've already started on the inside of the top, but I ran out of cedar. I see you brought some with you. The outside is to be in oak, and we shall have to obtain that, of course. How was your journey? Did you find Aunt and Uncle well?"

"We had a fine visit with them…and Deborah too. Your aunt and uncle asked much about you. You don't remember them, for we lived so long in Judea that we seldom saw them except at Passover time. Crowded conditions at those times prevented us from long visits—if any at all. They plan to come down here within a week, as your cousin Deborah is much in need of a change. I'm sure you remember our telling you that she lost her betrothed so tragically last year. She has been in deep grief ever since."

"I remember your talking about it. Something about Roman soldiers cutting off his hands and leaving him to bleed to death, wasn't it?" Reuben recalled. "Gruesome!"

"That's right. It was a terrible tragedy and waste. We must give them ample hospitality when they come. They have endured much."

"Are you pleased about the cabinet order, Father?" asked Reuben, anxious to keep the conversation on work. Some of his bitterness had left him now that he had seen Miriam twice that week, and he wanted to show himself as being responsible in the shop. Besides, he did not look forward to having the company, since it would take up more of his time and leave him with fewer opportunities to possibly see his beloved.

David noticed his reluctance to pursue the subject of the forthcoming visit, but decided to let the matter drop for the present. He and Johhebed had agreed that Reuben must find out for himself about the charming and beautiful Deborah.

The visit had really produced fruit in the way of the family's interest in an alliance between the two young people.

"David, you have come up with the same idea we had hoped for," declared his brother, Azariah, the father of Deborah. "Deborah has been morose and dejected for over a year now, and it's time something is done about it. There are many eligible young men in Capernaum, but she will have none of them. One of the sons of Zebedee, a fairly wealthy fisherman, has been smitten with her, but she will have no part of him. He is a godly young man too. This proposed visit to your home where she will see Reuben might bring her out of her grief and self-pity."

Rachel, David's sister-in-law upheld her husband's opinion. It was evident that this woman of large proportions was a bundle of nerves over concern for her daughter. She was only too willing to take advantage of this new opportunity which held such promise. Rachel had always been full of a natural humor, but her eyes now reflected sadness and her familiar smiles were absent. She had used food as a means of consolation, and her body was more than ample, giving her walk a type of waddle that reminded one of a fattened goose.

"I thank you for inviting us, David. And you too, Johhebed, of course. We have been apart too long. We would have been to see you before this, but right after you moved to Cana we began the house for Deborah and Caleb. Then there was his death, and of course, this last year has been like a bad dream. It will be nice to laugh a little again. It's been so long, my mouth may crack if I try."

"How do you think Reuben will feel about it all?" questioned Azariah of his brother.

"We can tell you this much without sounding prideful, I hope," answered David. "Reuben is a strong, handsome young man, both obedient and God fearing. We know he is rebellious over his own situation right now, but there's nothing we can do to help what has happened. Now we must take matters in our hands and seek another alliance. We want to see him married and settled down...and giving us grandchildren. But how about Deborah?"

As they sat together on heavy cushions on the floor, Azariah looked down at his feet for a moment, then raised his eyes and answered David. "There's no way of knowing how Deborah will react to this plan, but her mind cannot take much more depression. It's well worth a try."

David considered all of this as he and Reuben completed unloading the wood from his cart. He not only wondered about Deborah. He wondered about his own son. Why did the heart affect people to such an extent? Why could they not simply use common sense and get along with their lives when tragedy beset them? But, that's not the way it happens, he concluded. How would I react if something should befall Johhebed? God forbid!

"The countryside is beautiful up that way, Reuben," David said, still enthusiastic about the journey. "You have never been up that direction. Capernaum and the country around it is special. With the exception of the tax collector's booth just this side of the town and the attendant confusion, the scenery was splendid, and the fields were lush and productive. There was much grain, of course, and many orchards of date palms along with olive groves and a few vineyards. It is good fertile land.

"The Sea of Galilee is also beautiful and full of fish.

But there is something strange about it. Storms will often come up with no warning at all, especially in the daytime. The fishermen find it best to fish at night when the catches are more abundant.

"Well, enough of that for now. The Sabbath begins tonight, and we must hasten our work to be through by sundown. Your mother and Rhoda are already preparing food for this evening and tomorrow. We stopped at the market before we came home."

After unloading the cart, the men soon put away their tools and went home to perform their ritual cleansing. Following this, they perfumed their bodies with scented olive oil, put on clean tunics, and prepared for the Friday evening meal and the meeting at the synagogue. The Sabbath eve meal was always special. This day Johhebed had prepared roast goat, sweet fried cakes, figs brought from Capernaum and goat cheese. It was a joyful meal in honor of the Lord, and Johhebed and Rhoda were especially grateful that they would have rest until the following sundown. They would not even light a fire.

On the way to the synagogue that evening, David reflected that his son was not his usual sullen self which he had been since Nathan broke the betrothal. He wondered what had changed him, but determined to keep his silence. Surely he was more discreet than to have attempted to see Miriam, he thought. But David was wise enough to know that little—if anything—else would make him the least bit cheerful.

Reuben had been dealt a hard blow, and David knew that Reuben's friends were not making it easier for him. All except Nathanael, who appeared to be a sensitive, compassionate youth. They had been friends for two years, and both seemed devoted to God. Their many moments of levity and outdoor physical activity together gave their friendship a good balance. His other good friend and neighbor, Aaron, however, was congenial enough but had little depth. It pleased him to chide Reuben about Miriam at this difficult time, and Reuben did not appreciate it.

"When did you say our relatives from Capernaum are coming?" Reuben asked his father as they neared the synagogue.

"Within four days," David answered, trying not to sound as anxious as he felt. "Perhaps you can take some time off from the shop while they are here."

"Why me? Uncle Azariah is your brother, and you will want to visit with him. I can take care of things at the shop for you...just as I did the past few days."

"We'll see," David said flatly, as they arrived at the synagogue and sat down on the floor with the other men.

Miriam and Reuben had no way of getting together again after his family arrived home. The arrival of the house guests came only too quickly for Reuben. He hoped he wouldn't have to spend much of his time with them, but he did determine to be cordial.

Johhebed heard the cart pull up first at the noon hour and called to Rhoda to come greet her relatives. Rhoda was excited, for Deborah was a girl and they could spend time together, speaking of things girls like to talk about. She knew that Deborah was actually about Reuben's age, but she hoped they could be friends for a few days. What else would Deborah have to do during the visit, she wondered, other than listen to the older generation talk about boring subjects like taxes, work, Pontius Pilate, or such?

Rhoda could hardly wait to be beautiful and nubile like Deborah. Her visit with Deborah in Capernaum had given her a role model to emulate. She would ask many questions while she was in their home. Or so she thought. But her parents had other plans.

When David and Reuben came home late that afternoon, they saw the cart by the house and knew their guests had arrived. Going into the courtyard, they found them sitting under the shade of a canopy. David strode quickly to embrace his brother, sister-in-law and niece.

"It's wonderful to see you again so soon!" he exclaimed, smiling broadly. "We hope your journey was peaceful and uneventful."

"It was," Azariah assured him. "Few thieves await the traveler in the early morning."

"And this is Reuben," David said, turning towards his son with a grin. "It has been many a year since you have seen him. He and Deborah were but children when you last visited with us in Jerusalem. Deborah, this is Reuben, our son whom we talked about while we visited you."

Reuben managed to say, "Greetings, Deborah." But Deborah stood transfixed, looking at the tall young man before her. His bare arms, so tanned by the sun, revealed muscles only hard work and exercise could develop. His black wavy hair and piercing black eyes, along with a lean face and square jaw, completed the picture of a handsome figure.

"Greetings to you, Reuben," she finally managed and flashed him a beautiful smile. "It's been a very long time!"

The parents watched with suppressed interest and hopeful anticipation to see the reactions of both young people to each other. Obviously, Deborah was impressed by Reuben. Her face had not been so radiant for a year. Thus far, Reuben was impassive, but he was never one to make quick judgments of others.

"It's nice you and your parents are here, Deborah," he said simply. "Now will you excuse me while I wash up and change?" With that, Reuben turned and left.

The family, though disappointed in his quick departure, considered it only natural that he would wish to clean up after working most of the day. As time dragged on, however, and he did not return to join them all, Johhebed and David looked restlessly toward the doorway, obviously uncomfortable that he was taking an undue length of time to wash and slip on a clean tunic. Perhaps he is using special care since he is actually interested in the young woman, hoped Johhebed. But how could he help it, she deducted?

Deborah was an extremely beautiful young woman. She was tall, slim, with a tiny waist, full breasts and slim ankles. Her clothing left other dimensions to the imagination. Her hair was dark brown, straight, pulled back from her face and fastened in a twisted bun on the back of her neck. She had discarded the braids when she was betrothed to Caleb and had never returned to the custom because of her age, eighteen. Her facial features were finely chiseled and cameo-like. Her large brown eyes, edged with long, dark lashes, were sad but gleaming. Full lips gave her a seductive look, but it was apparent the girl had no guile. She was almost shy, but possessed a charming smile and an attractive innocence of expression.

When Reuben still did not come down from his room, David excused himself and went up to find out the reason. He found Reuben sitting on his pallet with his head in his hands, still unwashed and still in his soiled clothes.

"What is the matter with you, Reuben?" he demanded harshly. "You should have come down an hour ago. Our guests will certainly be hurt by your rudeness!"

"Why should they be?" inquired Reuben. "They have nothing to do with me. I cannot burden them with my troubles. You know that."

"Of course I do," the father said. "What has that to do with your being courteous to them? You can do that without bringing in your personal affairs. Besides, it's time you began putting your grieving aside and getting on with your life. Now wash up and come down and join us. I'll expect you quickly."

David got up and left, and Reuben slowly performed the cleansing and dressing, resenting the fact that he must talk with another girl when it was Miriam who was filling his heart with yearning. He was aware that Deborah was beautiful to the eye, but she was not Miriam. He wished she were not there.

After the evening meal, Johhebed and Rhoda insisted upon taking care of the dishwashing, while David took Azariah to meet with the other men in the village. Reuben wanted to join them, but David told him to stay with Deborah, since she needed someone to talk with. Perhaps he could cheer her up, he suggested. Rachel would want to visit with Johhebed.

"Deborah looks cheerful enough to me," said Reuben in whispered protest. David dismissed him with a wave of the hand as he and Azariah strode out of the courtyard.

Deborah was sitting on a cushion beside the fountain, looking ill at ease and downcast. When Reuben saw her he picked up a cushion and sat down near her. For a moment there was an awkward silence.

Reuben made some remarks about what his father had told him about the countryside around Capernaum, and she made some comparisons concerning the hilly regions around Cana. Then she boldly changed the subject.

"I guess you know why I am here," she said candidly. "I overheard Mama and Papa talking about it, and I assume you know too. I hope it doesn't upset you."

"I supposed it was because of the loss of your betrothed last year. I'm sorry about that. It must have been awful, but maybe this change will do you good. Naturally, it upsets me when someone else is unhappy. I'm unhappy too, you know."

"Yes, I heard what happened to you. Then we both have lost a loved one. Perhaps our parents' plan is a good one after all," she said, looking him in the eyes earnestly.

"I must have missed something. What plan?" he questioned cautiously, narrowing his eyes and returning her gaze with a puzzled one of his own.

"You mean you don't know? Oh, I'm sorry," she apologized anxiously, nervously rubbing the folds of her garment between her fingers. "Please forget that I said anything. It is of no consequence."

"No consequence? What do you mean no consequence?" he questioned, his eyes still narrowing and his head to one side. "If it is a good plan, as you say, it must be of some consequence."

"Please. As I said, I'm sorry to have spoken out of turn. Oh, here comes Rhoda," she warned. "Let us consider the subject closed."

Rhoda was followed by the two older women, and Reuben suggested they go up on the roof since the men would be returning soon. It also might be cooler there. He hoped Deborah would engage in conversation with the others. He had to think out what she had just said and try to piece the puzzle together. He could only hope to do that alone.

Deborah drew her aunt aside and was presumably talking with her about the view from the roof of the house. It was a view of beautiful hills and the beginnings of a magnificent sunset, accented by small fleecy clouds which took on all shades of pink, orange and even purple. A very tiny star was beginning to twinkle in the east. Reuben sat on a pillow near his aunt and Rhoda, ready to offer his cushion to one of the others when they joined them.

"I must speak with you, my aunt," said Deborah softly to Johhebed. "Just pretend we are looking around at the village."

"Of course, Deborah, but is something the matter? You do appear a bit worried," answered Johhebed as they looked out over the scene before them.

"It is Reuben," Deborah whispered. "He knows nothing about our plans...or rather your plans for us. You have not told him?"

"No, my child, we thought it best to wait and have you get acquainted first. He has been so upset about the other matter—his broken betrothal—that we felt it would be wiser not to say anything yet. We knew he would have no objection once he saw you. You are very beautiful, you know."

"Beauty is not everything. He confessed he is still unhappy. I started to say something about what our families had planned, but I could see he knew nothing about it. I'm really sorry. He is quite nice, and handsome."

"Do not fret, my dear. Reuben will come around. Your being here will be good for him. Now let us join the others. I hear David and your father returning."

Reuben jumped up and gathered enough cushions for all, reserving a place for his in back of the others. He might not listen to much of what his father would say this evening. He needed to straighten out the puzzle of his jumbled thoughts. A slight suspicion was forming in his mind, and he was appalled at what it might mean for him. Nothing must come between the love he and Miriam had for each other!

CHAPTER SIX

Pontius Pilate, governor of Judea was considered by many as an inept, spineless man who was always fearful of disapproval from Rome and exceedingly loyal to Tiberius. However, he was surprisingly supportive of the Jewish religious leaders and especially influenced by Herod, tetrarch of the Galilean region. In view of the open sedition in and around Jerusalem, Herod put his trust in these religious leaders to stop any rebellion.

Many Jews plotted rebellion against Rome and Caesar, as well as against their own rulers, and orderly collection of taxes was becoming impossible. The zealots, members of a militant Jewish sect, were behind much of this rebellion, but all the Jews spoke much of being victimized and highly burdened.

How long do you think Tiberius will live in seclusion in Capri?" asked David of Nathan one evening as they gathered with the other men of the village.

"Who knows?" answered Nathan. "I had high hopes for awhile, but he has turned into a degenerate like so many of the Romans. It is irksome to know that we are under his rule.

"By the way," he inquired, changing the subject, "how is your family? We have missed our close relationship. I know it is my fault, but I was hoping that we could put the betrothal thing behind us and go on with our friendship. It goes back a long way, you know."

David stroked his beard and held Nathan's gaze.

"Perhaps you are not having the problems we are having, Nathan. Reuben is so disconsolate that it has made life difficult for us. We thought recently he was coming out of it, as his attitude suddenly changed, but now he is bitter once more."

"That is to be regretted, of course, and I do understand. Miriam has been the same way...deeply depressed. We too thought she was getting over it recently, a few days ago, in fact, but now she is worse than ever. It seems that one of her friends told her yesterday morning at the well that she had seen Reuben with a very beautiful young woman when she passed by your house. They were standing by the gate, and a cart was being loaded in front. Miriam thought perhaps Reuben was going away with this young woman, but I'm sure you would have told me had it been so. It would have solved the problem, however, wouldn't it?" he added with a sly smile and a slight twinkle in his eyes.

"That shows how much you know about young lovers, Nathan!" David barked. "Your marriage was not consummated out of love, but Reuben and Miriam have deep feelings for one another. Those feelings are obviously not easily turned off, and we need to respect this.

However, I can explain the young woman with Reuben. She was Deborah, my niece from Capernaum, who was here with her parents at our invitation. To be truthful, I was—and still am—hoping for an alliance between Reuben and Deborah, but I can see that I tried to accomplish this too soon. She may be beautiful, but Reuben is still smitten with Miriam. We'll give it time, and perhaps it will work out. I have to respect your decision about them, even though I don't agree with it. I'm just sorry it all happened."

"We all are, but I do not change my mind. It would be fine if things would work out with your niece. I know you're anxious that Reuben marry and start a family. We, of course, wish the same for Miriam. Let's hope they each will find someone. I'm confident they will. Here comes Jonas," he interrupted as he saw their good friend approaching. "Ruth must be better today, as he has been staying home evenings while she was running a fever. Jonas is a good man—never complains, even though he and Ruth have so little."

The three men joined the others, and Nathanael announced that his friend, Philip, had just returned from the Jordon area where he had been hearing John. In fact, he had been baptized by him.

"Stop by the shop soon and tell us about it," asked David of him, not wishing to get into another altercation with Nathan.

"How about tomorrow morning?" Nathanael asked. "I'll bring in a broken bowl that needs fixing."

"Fine," said David, and switched immediately to another less controversial subject. Nathan had bristled at first, but said nothing to stir up feelings. With knitted brows, he mused on the repercussions of the broken betrothal. He remained firm in his feeling that he had done the right thing for his daughter. He simply had not anticipated such an intense reaction, nor did he expect that it would last long.

Nathanael arrived at David's shop early the following morning and embraced Reuben when he came in. The young men had been congenial from the first time they met two years previous in the synagogue school. They sat in the room where the Torah scrolls were kept and prepared their lessons under the strict supervision of the hazzan, keeper of the scrolls. Reuben had observed that Nathanael was especially devout, excelling in his ability to learn. He looked up to him and was eager to cultivate his friendship. This friendship had taken them through two journeys to Jerusalem at Passover with their families, as well as frequent physical games of skill in the streets with other boys in the village. Both had a special love for music and relished playing their flutes as others danced in the streets.

"Sit down, Nathanel," said David, dusting off his hands and indicating a stool. "I want you to tell me everything you can about your friend Philip's stay in the lower Jordan valley—the part about John the Baptist, I mean. You know, of course, that my wife and I are quite interested in the man. This has caused much heartbreak for Reuben, as I am sure he has confided in you. But Reuben knows that his mother and I have a right to our convictions. We don't expect Reuben to follow him, but we feel strongly about what the man preaches. Now, just what did your friend tell you when you saw him?"

"He came through here two days ago on his way back to Bethsaida. That's the long way around, you know, but he was in hopes of getting me to go down and hear this John. I laughed at him, of course. He understands that I meant no offense, but I devoutly believe what our fathers and their fathers—on back to the patriarchs—have taught us. John has brought out some things which stir up some of the people," said Nathanael earnestly.

"What for instance?" inquired David.

"Well, he believes that the hour of judgment has already come upon the people, and that another would follow him who would bring in a new era," Nathanael related. "He seems to chastise our religious leaders for failure to repent. That's something I cannot understand. If we cannot follow and trust our religious leaders, who then can we trust?"

"We trust our God, Nathanael. 'In him do we trust.' Did not the psalmist tell us that? The psalmist also told us that we are deep in sin. Do not our religious leaders often speak one way and act another? I do not refer to our rabbi, of course, but we have heard things from Jerusalem about high priests. Annas was an unscrupulous schemer before he was deposed, and I hear he is still in league with his son-in-law, Caiaphas. I trust neither of them," David snorted, his black eyes blazing.

"But consider something, Nathanael," he continued. "I have not even told Reuben this, but now is as good a time as any. Johhebed and I have spoken of returning to the lower Jordan valley and taking Rhoda and Reuben with us. Would you join us? We would also go to Jericho."

Before Nathanel could answer, Reuben jumped to his feet from the crude bench on which he sat and all but shouted, "What do you mean by including me in such a journey, Father? Hasn't enough harm already been done because of that man? I cannot even consider it," he added more softly with his head bowed. His grief once more overwhelmed him, and he tightened his fists.

"Reuben, you are still my son, and I feel it would be only fair for you to listen to the man and see why your mother and I feel as we do. You will never understand us until you do. I say the whole family is going, and I know that I'm right in insisting upon it. And the invitation is still open for you, Nathanael."

"Thank you, David, sir, but I did promise Philip that I would accompany him if I ever decided to go. He plans to return again soon," Nathanael explained. "But I can understand why you want Reuben to go. No offense meant, Reuben," he added, turning to look at his friend. "It might give him a much better understanding of his own situation."

"I can understand your desire to go with Philip, Nathanael," David offered. "We'll speak more of this later, Reuben," and he turned back to his work. "I must continue to plan the chest which Jahdai ordered. Thank you for stopping by, Nathanael."

Nathanael left the wooden bowl to be mended and bade his friends farewell.

"Father, are you truly serious about us all going down to the Jordan to hear John?" asked Reuben incredulously. "Are you trying to completely ruin our friendship with Nathan and the family?"

"No, my son, that is far from the case," denied David, stopping his work. "Nathan cannot impose his conscience upon mine. And in all fairness to you—and to me—in view of what you have recently suffered and are so resentful about, I sincerely believe it would be well for you to at least listen to the Baptist. I am hoping it will give you an understanding of your mother and me."

Reuben carefully measured a small piece of wood to make a handle for a tool they were working on and was silent for awhile. He was obviously considering what his father had said, for his brows were knitted together and the corners of his mouth turned down in a scowl. Finally, he raised his head and somberly looked David straight in the eyes.

"All right, Father. Perhaps you are right. But can we at least keep quiet about our journey? It would break Miriam's heart...further, I mean...if she found out about it."

"Well, I do have some trading to do anyway. Thus far, no caravans have been through here with any oak lately. And we need some olive wood, also. I'll pick up some camel hide for Nathan since he mentioned his low supply."

Johhebed and Rhoda were advised of the plans and it was decided that they would leave in three days, immediately after the Sabbath. This would still give David sufficient time to cut and carve the oak chest when he returned. It was important that he obtain the wood as soon as possible. He could mend Nathanael's bowl in the meantime, along with a few other small jobs. David was conscientious with his work, but right now he felt the burden of his son's spiritual life, as well as the unity of his family.

"Who will run your shop while you're gone, David?" asked Irnehash the following evening when David announced that he was taking his family with him to Jericho. David mentioned that he knew a merchant there who sold wood, and he was sure he could locate camel hide for Nathan.

"I can close my shop. Without proper wood, I cannot run it, and the last few caravans through here carried mainly spices and oil. I need the oil, of course, to rub into the wood, but my shop is useless without a variety of wood," he answered. "Reuben needs to learn what to look for and how to bargain."

David did not wish to carry the conversation further, for he knew he would be boxed into a corner concerning going to the Jordan wilderness area. And he refused to lie. Changing the subject quickly, he turned to Jonas with a smile.

"How is Ruth these days? We see you more often, so she must be doing well—or at least better."

"She is, I am grateful to say," said Jonas, love for his wife showing in his expressive eyes. "She is all I have, you know. After losing our daughter, our son became rebellious and later joined the Zealots. I don't know what got into him—but then you've heard this story enough before. Forgive me for repeating myself."

"It is nothing, my friend. In fact, it's good to clear the mind with someone else. Holding something inside, especially grief or anger, festers and will destroy," answered David. "Do you ever hear from Enos?" he added.

"It has been fully a year," said Jonas flatly. "He came home then for food for the men in his band who had been with him fighting in the hills nearby. They were headed for Caesarea and came upon a troop of Roman soldiers. There was a skirmish, but the Romans overpowered them. Their resentment of Roman control burns hotly in their breasts, and they tried hard to get me to stir up our villagers. But I refused. It would only lead to bloodshed, and Ruth and I worry enough about his safety. But, it does no good. He has chosen his way of life, and we seem to have no influence over him. He appears to have put all thoughts of God out of his mind."

"I'm sorry, Jonas. I pray he will be protected until he realizes that violence will not solve his problems—the Jews' problems, that is. The zealot, Judas of Galilee, will be remembered for his ill-fated revolt against the Romans, when all of his followers were dispersed. But these others must pay no heed."

"This is true. The Romans cannot be overpowered by small bands of men. Messiah will be our deliverer from oppression. Why does he not come, I wonder?"

The talk continued along that vein until sunset.

There was no opportunity for Reuben to see Miriam again before he left for Jericho with his family. His heart was aching, and every fiber of his being cried out to see her. It seemed so unfair! He understood his father's reasoning in wanting him to go, but his emotions would not accommodate reason. Every day away from her was almost more than he could bear. He would beat his breast when alone at night and plead with God to bring them together again. Now he would be a far distance away, with not the slightest possibility of any kind of communication. What is she doing? he wondered. What is she thinking? Does she want to be near me as much as I want to be near her? What if her father found someone else for her to marry? The thoughts kept crowding in on him like a vise until he could barely endure.

The morning of their departure came, and dark clouds filled the sky. The parched earth was in need of water, and David hoped for rain because of their crops. There had been little work to be done in the fields lately due to the drought. Perhaps when they returned, Reuben and Jonas could get to the fall planting. But not without rain.

The family of four, along with their spare clothing, left little room in the cart. The two donkeys, Saul and Samson, would have to work hard on the hills until they reached the plain of Jezreel.

"How long will it take us to get to Jericho?" inquired Rhoda, excited about the journey ahead of her. "It seemed like a long time when we were there before."

"About four days, my child," answered David, "unless the weather becomes bad and the roads are muddy. Let's not consider that now, however. I think we can count on four days. I have walked it in that time, and we made it in four days the last time we made the journey."

He turned to Johhebed and said, "Since we're going through Nazareth, do you wish to stop and greet your cousin Mary?"

"I would like to briefly visit with her, David, if you don't mind. It has been such a long time for me, you know. But we will not linger," she promised. "The family was away the last time we came through…remember? A neighbor said they had gone to a funeral."

"Can I run to the carpenter's shop and see Jesus?" inquired Reuben eagerly. "I should like very much to see him—only for a moment, as Mother says."

"Yes, only for a moment," agreed David, happy that something would dispel his son's gloom.

The cart bumped slowly on, swaying with the uneven gait of the donkeys and the ruts in the road, which twisted and turned on its way to Nazareth. The cloud cover remained fairly still, mercifully shielding them from the hot rays of the sun.

Reaching Nazareth, they tethered the animals outside Mary's modest house as Reuben took off running toward the carpenter shop of the cousin to whom he was so strongly drawn. Mary, beaming with delight that her relatives had come, welcomed them warmly and bid them come inside and visit.

"We really can't stay, Mary," said Johhebed, after embracing her cousin. "It's wonderful to see you, but we're on our way to Jericho and we have a long way to go, as you know. Reuben just went to the carpenter shop to see Jesus, and we shall have to leave when he returns."

"Jesus is away," said Mary solemnly. A look of anticipation came over her face, and she added, "He has gone to see our cousin John, who is preaching by the Jordan near Jericho. Perhaps you will see him. He did not say when he would return, but he acts strangely at times—as if he had much on his mind. He is a good man and cares well for me. I can only love him...not understand him. No mother could ask for a better son."

"Why did he never marry?" inquired Johhebed. "He sounds as if he would have made a good husband for some fortunate young woman."

"He never mentioned it himself," said Mary wistfully. "And when Joseph and I brought it up when he was much younger, he said it was not meant to be for him. As I told you, one cannot always understand him. He speaks with such authority that I have demanded little of him. It is as though he were leading me."

Just then Reuben returned. When told where Jesus had gone, he joined the family in expressing hope they would meet up with him on the road or in the Jordan area. The family then embraced Mary and left.

The cart twisted and creaked along the tenacious curves, down the narrow ridge south of the city until cone-shaped Mount Tabor came into view, rising from the plain of Jezreel.

"This old cart wouldn't make it up there!" voiced Reuben, happy to be on more level ground.

"Saul and Samson will have a better time of it from now on to Jericho," said David, relieved to be off the dangerous cliffs around Nazareth. "We'll cross the Jordan River at Beth-shan to avoid the unwelcome reception we would no doubt receive from the Samaritans. Herod governs Peraea, and we are more protected there. You brought water, didn't you, Johhebed?" he asked, turning to his wife.

"Yes. Rhoda, hand your father a water jug," she requested the sleepy-eyed girl. "We could all use a bit, I think."

The cart continued on slowly until nightfall. After David and Reuben watered the donkeys in a nearby stream, they performed the daily task of greasing the axles of the cart. Then David led his family in a petition to God for their safety. In their traveling home, they fell into an exhausted sleep. It was uncomfortable, but their tired bodies welcomed the stillness and opportunity to stretch out a bit on top of their extra clothing. Reuben's last thoughts before dropping off to sleep were of Miriam and the feel of her soft lips upon his. It was almost real, and he smiled as he drifted into a dreamless euphoria of sleep.

For two more days they traveled uneventfully. The Jordan crossing, a source of anxiety for David, was accomplished easily due to the dry season. David and Reuben assisted the animals in negotiating the crossing, splashing water on them to cool them off.

At one point of the journey, a scorching khamsin blew in from the desert on the east, and the oppressive heat would have made travel too much for them had David not been prepared for such an emergency. He kept a roll of the goat's hair cloth used for tents which he had once bought from a tentmaker. With the use of poles and ropes, he was able to provide a windbreaker on one side of the cart to use as a buffer against the harsh wind and dust.

The fourth day arrived, and they found themselves in the dense jungle of brush, shrubs and tamarisk trees in the zor. The road was narrow, but it was strangely filled with travelers—mainly on foot.

"Why are there so many people around here?" David asked one elderly man, bent in frame and using a heavy stick to assist in walking.

"They are going to hear the one called John. He is preaching close to here today, it is said," answered the wayfarer.

"Have you heard him?" inquired David, excitement rising within him.

"Only once," the man answered. "But I feel drawn to return."

"Here, let me help you into our cart, and we'll take you the rest of the way," said David kindly, offering the man his hand to help him up. "What is your name?"

"Samuel. I come from Amathus. Thank you for your kindness. I was getting weary."

Rueben moved over to make room for him, and Samuel smiled appreciatively.

The crowd thickened as the family plodded along on the rocky ground. Reuben put out his hand to steady the stranger riding with them. He looked so old and fragile to the young man.

Two horses carrying Roman soldiers rode by and all but crowded them off the road. There was something less arrogant about these centurions. They even nodded and smiled slightly as they passed the slow-moving cart.

"What are they doing here?" inquired David angrily. "Are we to expect trouble?"

"Oh, no," Samuel assured him. "Many Roman soldiers have come to hear this man—Pharisees too—and a high priest was present when I was here before. Notice the people on the road. They are all types. Some could even be the tax collectors—and some prostitutes. Station in life seems to mean nothing when it comes to the soul."

"That is true," considered David. "But the Romans surely don't believe in our God."

"Some might now," said Samuel thoughtfully. "You have not heard the Baptist before?"

"Once, just as you, but only a few were present then. We were much touched by his preaching and want to hear him again. That crowd over there—that must be where he is preaching today," said David further. It was on the bank of the Jordan River, and some people were in the water near the shore.

David stopped the donkeys and proceeded to unhitch them and lead them down to the shore to drink before gathering his family together to join the nearby crowd.

Samuel climbed out with Reuben's help and went on, eager to hear the words of John.

Reuben was despondent. He had no desire to be part of that crowd, and no desire to hear the man who was becoming so renowned in Galilee, Peraea, Judea, and perhaps other areas. He could not help feeling an actual resentment toward this man, who had been the reason behind his separation from Miriam. And yet he knew he must go out of respect for his mother and father. He helped Johhebed and Rhoda out of the cart, but remained silent and stood off by himself.

David tethered Saul and Samson to a small shade tree and strode over to his family in an exuberant manner, obviously anxious to go down to the large group by the water.

"Come, let us join the others," he said jovially. "The crowd is growing larger."

Noticing Reuben still standing there as the family started to walk toward the river's edge, David shouted, "Reuben, come!"

Reuben's somber eyes gazed at his father, and he reluctantly uprooted himself from the spot and dragged along behind the others. He noticed a long-haired and bearded man of about thirty years standing in the shallow part of the river, lowering an older person into the water and speaking some words at the same time. This must be the baptizing which was spoken of. Others waited in line a short distance away.

Reuben had never seen a baptism, as it was an infrequent ceremony with the Jews and took place only when a gentile was converted to the Jewish faith in God. This would be a rarity indeed in Cana. He knew about or had taken part in the ritual cleansings, which were occasioned weekly on Sabbath eve and after such things as touching a dead person, or being healed from leprosy. However, these were usually done away from the public view.

"Oh, generation of vipers, who has warned you to flee from the wrath to come?" the strong voice of John thundered, as Reuben came within hearing distance.

What does he mean? Reuben wondered. Why is he calling the people a generation of vipers? Does he mean me, too? Huh!

"Bring forth therefore fruits worthy of repentance, and begin not to say within yourselves, 'We have Abraham as our father,' for I say to you that God is able of these stones to raise up children unto Abraham," the man continued, eyes blazing and arms outstretched.

Raise up children from the stones? Reuben questioned. The man is a lunatic! Nathan was surely right about him.

"And now also the axe is laid unto the root of the trees: every tree therefore which does not bring forth good fruit is hewn down, and cast into the fires."

"What shall we do then?" some people in the crowd shouted.

"He that has two coats, let him give to him that has none, and he that has meat, let him do likewise."

"Hmmm," said Reuben aloud to himself. "That makes sense. At least, it would be a good way to live. Miriam is that sort of a person—full of kindness for others in need."

"What did you say, son" asked David hearing Reuben speak.

"Oh, er, nothing," Reuben replied in a low voice, his face flushing a bit as he turned toward his father who had stepped back beside him.

"Let's go in a little closer," suggested David. This time Reuben was willing to go.

Some publicans came to be baptized and asked John, "Master, what shall we do?"

"Collect no more than that which is ordered you," demanded John.

A group of soldiers standing nearby asked of him, "And what shall we do?"

"Do violence to no man, neither accuse any falsely, and be content with your wages, the Baptist commanded.

Murmuring was heard throughout the crowd as the people wondered aloud if John were the Messiah—the Christ.

The rugged man of the wilderness wearing a tunic of camel's hair with a leather girdle around his loins, perceived what the crowd was questioning and with piercing eyes and strong countenance looked about and said, "I indeed baptize you with water, but one mightier than I comes: the straps of whose sandals I am not worthy to unloose. He shall baptize you with the Holy Ghost and with fire: whose fan is in his hand, and he will thoroughly purge his floor, and will gather the wheat into his garner; but the chaff he will burn with unquenchable fire."

He continued to exhort the people concerning their sins and the need for repentance.

Reuben gazed around and suddenly saw his cousin, Jesus, coming toward the crowd. He called, "Jesus!" and started to hasten over to him, but David stayed him with a hand on his arm.

"Do not cause a commotion, son, advised David. "Perhaps this cousin of yours has business with John."

"Yes, you are probably right, Father," acknowledged Reuben. "Mary did say he was coming here to see him." But Reuben kept his eyes on him.

John, seeing Jesus coming toward him said, "Behold the Lamb of God, who takes away the sins of the world. This is he of whom I said, 'After me comes a man who is preferred before me; for he was before me.' And I knew him not: but that he should be manifest to Israel, therefore am I come baptizing with water."

Reuben and David saw Jesus go down to the water and heard him ask to be baptized. Then a strange thing happened. John refused him saying, "I have need to be baptized by you, and you come to me?"

"Permit it to be so now," demanded Jesus, "for thus it is fitting for us to fulfill all righteousness."

"What is Jesus saying?" asked Reuben of his father. "What does he mean that it will fulfill all righteousness? Who is Jesus to say this? He is simply a carpenter from Nazareth. I am confused."

"Wait and listen, son," said David, his eyes alight and excitement showing in his face.

The crowd watched Jesus being baptized, many unaware of the conversation which had taken place between him and John. As he came up out of the water, the clouds in the sky parted, opening the heavens above him. The sun shone through, and a dove came down and lighted upon his shoulder.

Reuben then barely distinguished thunderous words from above saying, "This is my beloved Son, in whom I am well pleased." He stood rooted to the ground as if in shock. His face paled, and his eyes sought those of his father. Visibly shaken, he questioned soberly, "What does it all mean?"

CHAPTER SEVEN

"This is my beloved Son, in whom I am well pleased."

Could I have actually heard those very words? pondered Reuben, unnerved by such a revelation. Was it purely imagination? But how could I even imagine such an awesome thought, especially when it concerned my own cousin, a mere carpenter in Nazareth? Galilee was not held in high esteem by people of Judea because it was inhabited by both gentiles and Jews. An unlikely place to harbor Messiah!

Surely, his thought continued, Jesus could not be the Messiah for whom we all await so eagerly! He would be King of the Jews, and Jesus...well...he was hardly a king!

"Father..."Reuben's voice was hoarse and cracked as he tried to speak, turning to David for some sort of explanation. "Did you hear a voice from above just now? Just after Jesus came up out of the water?"

But David was clearly shaken, and his face was ashen as he turned to his son.

"I...I...don't know, son. I did...hear something, but I was just wondering if I imagined it. I made out the words 'beloved Son,' but the rest was more of a rumble. Let's ask your mother and sister if they heard anything."

Retreating back a ways from the edge of the water, the men joined Johhebed and Rhoda who were seated at the foot of a tamarisk tree.

"Did you just hear anything unusual—from up above?" asked David offhandedly, not wanting to repeat what he thought he heard until someone else confirmed it. He actually felt foolish in asking, but his heart was beating rapidly. Reuben's eyes were riveted upon his mother's seeking confirmation of the strange occurrence. His heart, too, beat fast, and he was inwardly moved.

"No, David, except for a brief rumble of thunder. Then all was quiet. Perhaps that was unusual for this time of year. David, you look pale. Do you feel well?"

"I'm all right, my love. Perhaps the excitement of all of this on top of the journey got to me. We haven't eaten, you know." He could not tell her what he thought he had heard if she hadn't heard it also. It sounded insane. But Reuben...he heard it!

Wiping his brow with the back of his hand, David turned to his son and soberly suggested that they return to the shore.

"But, I must find Jesus," said Reuben. "I wish to speak with him, and he seems to have left the shore."

"All right, son. We will be right here."

Reuben glanced around through the crowd before starting off to locate his cousin. But it was impossible to pick out individuals gathered around the Baptist. He strode off in the direction of the gathering, straining to find Jesus. Children were running and playing games on the periphery of the adult populace. One ragged and dirty urchin, shouting and looking the other way at a playmate, bumped into him.

"Ugh...I didn't see you," the boy said, grinning. He was gone as quickly as he had appeared.

Reuben encountered a strange mixture of people— rich and poor, feeble-minded and intelligent-looking, crippled and robust. Two Pharisees stood idly by, conversing with each other with drawn and pious expressions.

"This man insists upon self-immersion to signify cleansing from sin," said one. "Does he not know that we keep the law at all times and need no such cleansing! Yet he looked straight at us!"

"I saw him," agreed the other. "Do you think we should report him as a troublemaker? On the other hand, if the people feel he is right about the Messiah..."

"Don't be a fool!" exhorted his friend. "How could a man like that know anything about Messiah? Look!" he continued, pointing to a group of Roman soldiers pushing their way to the shore. "That is all we need now...more trouble from the Romans!"

Reuben inched his way through the concentrated mass of people, most of whom were intent upon the preacher in the water. He knew that Jesus had left the water at a nearby point and felt that he must be close at hand.

"Behold the Lamb of God!" John was saying, and no one paid attention to Reuben.

"Have you seen the one who was just baptized?" asked Reuben of a young Jew with a scarred but kindly face.

"I saw him go that way," he answered, pointing in the opposite direction from which Reuben had come.

For an hour Reuben searched, but to no avail. It was as though Jesus had disappeared immediately after the water ritual. Finally, Reuben's conscience smote him about leaving his family for so long, and he returned to them. He did see Samuel and offered him a ride to Jericho, but the elderly man was headed back to his home town.

"Do you think that could have been the Messiah?" Samuel asked with a haunted look on his face. "John said this man would baptize us with the Holy Ghost. Who else but Messiah would do that?"

"I am confused, Samuel. I wish I understood it all. Perhaps we shall some day."

"I'm ready now," answered Samuel feebly and hobbled on.

Reuben rejoined his family and told them he was unable to locate Jesus anywhere. They were eating bread and fruit they had brought with them when David announced that it would be wise to proceed to Jericho and stop again to hear John on their return journey.

"Perhaps Jesus will be here then," he conjectured, turning to Reuben. "I rather hope so myself," he added in a low and barely audible voice.

Travel was heavy on the way to Jericho. The crossing at the ford of the Jordan was made with much difficulty. Although the river was fairly low, Samson and Saul had trouble pulling the cart crosswise to the current—often stumbling on the rocks on the river bottom. David and Reuben got out and led them, but other travelers jostled them in eagerness to reach the opposite side quickly. Common courtesy was lacking in many of the people from the myriad walks of life. Occasionally a kind face appeared and smiled, making room for them to pass, but such was a rarity.

At one point of the crossing an irate and fleshy man came charging up behind them, venting expletives in the direction of David.

"I was listening to John," he exploded, "and when I came back to the spot where I left my basket of bread and cheese, the basket was empty. Some urchins told me your asses had eaten the food! Now I have no lunch!"

"Oh, I'm sorry, forgive me for this. I thought I had tied the donkeys securely. We still have some bread and fruit in our cart. Please have some of ours." Reaching into the cart, he pulled out his own basket and handed the red-faced man a piece of bread and some well-ripened grapes. Rhoda stifled a giggle at the thought of the donkeys eating the man's lunch.

"I'll take the bread," said the surly stranger, "but not that rotten fruit! Even the asses wouldn't eat that!" He turned and left, eagerly gulping the bread.

"Not even a thank you," muttered Johhebed. "If one is truly hungry, ripe fruit doesn't matter."

"He was more angry than hungry," said David. "I have yet to find a way to make a donkey be polite. On with you, Saul and Samson!" he shouted, giving the animals a slap on their rumps. "We'll fill you up when we find a stable in Jericho. You may not have bread and cheese, but it should be good donkey fare."

Once on the other shore of the Jordan, David and Reuben rode silently for awhile in the front of the cart, each deep in thought about what they had seen and heard in the zor area of the wilderness where John was preaching.

David contemplated some of the prophesies of Isaias, which spoke of a voice crying in the wilderness, preparing the way for the Lord. He deeply desired to share these things with his family, but needed to be certain before he did. How could he be certain? Jesus was surely one of the last persons he would have considered as being Messiah. Where was he to be born? The prophet Micah indicated Bethlehem Ephratah in Judea—the birthplace of King David.

His heart beat a little faster as he searched his memory. He had lived in the area near Bethlehem when Johhebed's cousin, Mary, had her first child. She had come with her husband, Joseph, to be taxed at the time of the census, as Joseph was in the lineage of David. That must have been twenty-five or thirty years ago, before he and Johhebed even knew each other, much before they were married. But she had told him something, and he had dismissed it as just another story of one of her relatives. One thing he did remember, however, was that the baby was born in a stable, with animals around him. Would a king be born in that fashion? Hardly! But a nagging feeling kept disturbing his thoughts. He must search the Scriptures when they returned to Cana—if only to prove that he was wrong in this new train of thought spawned by John.

Reuben was likewise contemplating the time spent listening to John and seeing Jesus baptized. He did not know as much prophecy as his father, but he did know what he saw and heard. He could not understand some of the things John was saying, particularly about the religious leaders, but he knew that his own life was not without some of the sins John mentioned. He did agree with the philosophy and teaching about one's relationship with his fellow man.

Perhaps Father was right in making me come, he considered, but how would all this fit in with Miriam? Even though their betrothal was broken, he knew he could marry no other person. In the slim hope they would ever get together again, how would she approve of his feelings about John the Baptist? Right now he was willing to forego those feelings for her love. He promised himself that nothing could come in the way of that!

But what about Jesus? he pondered. Could he possibly...by the wildest stretch of the imagination... be?...No, of course not. He must put such a thought out of his mind entirely. It simply could not be.

The cart creaked, wobbled and bumped along the rugged road toward their destination. Wild dogs would often come close and snarl at them, baring their sharp fangs as they growled and nipped at the legs of the donkeys. Their loose skin revealed their ribs, indicating that they were indeed hungry. Reuben found a few morsels to toss at them, diverting their attention for a short span. Rhoda recoiled at the snakes slithering across the road from time to time. All rejoiced that they had the cart. All but Samson and Saul who stopped short each time.

At the sight of the first olive grove, the four rejoiced even more. The heat was oppressive as they were going downhill and getting closer to the level of the Salt Sea. The atmosphere was not humid, but the dry heat was more like an oven than any place they had known.

"Oh, look!" cried Rhoda, pointing her finger ahead. There are palm trees! I remember those from the time we came before. So many of them together. It's beautiful! Will the dates be ripe?"

"Oh, yes," said Johhebed, "and we will pick some and some olives too, if the owners say we can. Usually, they cannot pick them all and are only too happy for others to have some."

Upon entering the city they saw a potter sitting at his wheel, turning it with his feet placed on a wooden collar, the wheel sitting in a hole in the ground.

"Shalom!" hailed David. "It's a hot day to be working like that!"

"If I do not work, I do not eat...or pay my taxes to Caesar. Is it not so?"

"It is indeed so, my friend. Be in peace."

The family found the marketplace, and David immediately looked for the dealer in various kinds of wood. Johhebed and Rhoda spied a stand which displayed beautiful linens woven from flax grown in the area and dyed in many colors. Perhaps they could buy some the next morning. Reuben took care of the cart and the donkeys, finding a stable for the night, and then went to meet his father.

It was late in the day and most of the dealers were closing up their stands, hoping for a respite from the intense heat. They were sweaty and tired, but they did not grumble at the possibility of a sale. After David had made a deal concerning some choice pieces of oak and olive wood, and had bargained with another man for camel hide for Nathan, he and Reuben carried the bundles to the cart parked by the stable. David gave the stable keeper a denarius to watch the cart overnight. He received a toothless grin and a bow of the head in thanks and confirmation. David did not know which smelled the worst—the man or the camel hide.

The family sought and found an inn for the night. All slept peacefully until a raucous group came in around midnight and was thrown out an hour later by the innkeeper's wife, who called them names that did not bear repeating. She was a woman of ample dimensions, and Reuben thought he would not wish to incur her disfavor. Finally, the place was quiet once more, until the screeching of fighting cats invaded their slumber, reminding them that Jericho was famed for its feline population. The four Galileans decided it would be good to return to the relative serenity of their own home.

Back in Cana, in the meantime, the sleep of Nathan and Esther was disturbed for another reason. Miriam.

Since Reuben's departure with his family, Miriam had grown more and more withdrawn. When Nathan announced that David and Johhebed were going to Jericho to buy wood, she had hoped wildly that Reuben might stay home and they could meet once more in the grove of Zipporah. The old woman was still not well and Miriam went daily to help her. But Jacob brought news that Reuben had accompanied his family, and she was desolate. To make things worse, her family was discussing various possibilities of a future husband for her. She was unable to impress upon them the fact that she wanted no other husband than Reuben. Her father would glare at her and invariably inform her that he and her mother knew what was best for her life. And that would end the discussion.

One night Miriam awoke with a fast heartbeat, a numbness in her arm, and a feeling that there was a tight band around her head. She even felt a huge knot in her stomach, and she broke out in a cold sweat from fright. She wondered if she were dying and cried out for her mother to come.

"What is the matter, dear one?" cried Esther, having rushed into Miriam's room at the first sound of her voice. She lit the lamp by Miriam's pallet and the eerie light revealed wide-eyed fear on the girl's face. "Did you perhaps have a bad dream?"

"No, Mama," Miriam said weakly. "I feel like I am dying. I feel bad all over. I never felt this way before. My heart races and my head…"

"Nathan, come quickly!" Esther shouted.

Throwing on a tunic, Nathan sleepily joined his wife and daughter. But all feeling of sleep disappeared when he saw his beloved Mim. He knew immediately she was actually ill.

"I will boil some herbs," said Esther in panic. It was all she knew to do, though she was at a loss to know which herbs to boil for the symptoms Miriam displayed. She had felt the girl's face and there was no fever. It was all very strange. But she hastened downstairs to do what she could.

Nathan tried to soothe the pain in Miriam's head by rubbing it, and indeed his presence had a calming effect upon her.

"Am I dying, Papa?" asked Miriam feebly. "Is this what it is like to die?"

"You are not dying," reassured Nathan, wishing he could be reassured himself. "You are not feverish, so perhaps you are reacting from a particularly bad dream."

"I dreamed nothing," answered Miriam weakly. "But your hand does feel good upon my forehead. Please keep on rubbing it."

"I'll rub it for hours if need be, my daughter. Soon your mother will bring you the herbal potion to drink, which should help you. Tell me, have you ever felt this way before?"

"No, Papa," she said, beginning to relax under the ministrations of Nathan. "But, please don't leave me. I don't want to be alone."

"You won't have to be alone, Mim. Either your mother or I will stay with you until you are feeling better."

Esther finally returned with two small cups of liquid for Miriam to drink. Not knowing what to fix, she had mixed several herbs together—anise, mint, and rue, flavored with pomegranate juice—which she gave Miriam to drink first. Nathan held his arm across the back of her shoulders as she sipped the potion, and then Esther handed her the second cup which contained wine and myrrh to alleviate the pain and help her to sleep. Nathan eased her back down on the pallet and resumed rubbing her forehead and the back of her neck. She soon became drowsy and sleep overtook her.

"One of us must stay with her," said Nathan to his wife. "I promised her she would not be alone."

"Let me stay now, Nathan, so you can get your rest. You will need it for the coming day. I can lie down on the floor beside Miriam and will hear her if she becomes restless. I've always slept lightly since the children were born. Besides, your snoring might wake her. Sometimes I imagine a pig is grunting in my ear when I awake—but it's only you snorting in your sleep!"

"Why, I never!" She stopped him with a giggle and they embraced before he went to their room to try and return to sleep. It was not easy, for he was deeply disturbed over his daughter's plight, wondering just what caused her obvious illness.

Esther dozed fitfully on the floor beside her daughter, waking often and checking the girl's breathing. Each time she was assured that Miriam was deep in sleep, and she too wondered about it all. She felt weary and lethargic when she dragged her body up off the floor in the early morning, awakening Jacob to sit with his sister until she could return to the room.

In response to the sleepy-eyed boy's question as to why he must sit with Miriam, Esther merely told him that she was ill and must not be alone. She then went down to start the fire in her oven for the morning's baking. Then she ran to the well to draw water before others congregated and would ask why Miriam wasn't there. After coming back, she quickly made up her dough and rushed upstairs to her still-sleeping daughter's room.

"You need to awaken your father," she told Jacob, "and then gather some more wood. Our supply is getting low for the oven. The goat needs milking, too. I must stay with Miriam until she awakens at least. Your father can sit with her while I bake the bread."

Miriam finally stirred and Esther put her hand on the girl's arm and inquired how she felt.

"I am better, Mama," she answered groggily, turning her head to look at her mother and smiling wanly. "Whatever you gave me must have helped a lot. I do feel strange, though. I feel as though I were there in that corner and looking over here. It's hard to explain."

Tears began to trickle down the girl's cheeks and soon she was sitting up and sobbing convulsively.

"Miriam, my dear, I'm sure that you're going to be all right. But if crying helps, then by all means cry."

She knelt down, putting her arms around her daughter, and Miriam responded by desperately clinging to her mother. Fear once more revealed itself on her face and her racking sobs brought Nathan into the room.

"Just how is she, Esther? Why is she sobbing so?" he asked anxiously, joining his wife at the girl's bedside and stroking the top of her head.

"She seemed better when she first awoke, but now this. I don't understand it all, but if you will stay with her, I'll go down and bake the bread and set out the fruit and cheese so you and Jacob can eat. He's gone to milk the goat and will bring back fresh milk for you."

Esther released her embrace and planted a kiss on Miriam's cheek.

"I'll be back as soon as I bake the bread. Do you feel like eating?"

"No, Mama, not now."

Her sobbing diminished and she lay back down on her pallet, staring up at the ceiling. She watched a spider crawl across it and disappear in a crack in the corner. I wish I could disappear like that, she thought. Why can't I just disappear? Even Reuben might not know I was gone, nor even miss me.

"Do you want to tell me why you were crying, Mim?" asked Nathan softly. "Is your head bothering you again?"

"No, Papa, it's not my head. I don't know what it is. I just felt like crying for no reason that I know of."

"I hope it isn't Reuben again. But we'll speak of that later. Right now I want you to stay quiet for awhile. I must go down and eat my meal with Jacob, but your mother will be up as soon as she serves it."

He patted her hand and started to leave.

"Oh, please don't go, Papa. I don't want to be alone. I'm afraid."

"What are you afraid of, daughter? There is nothing to fear. You are perfectly safe here in our home, and you can call out if you need us."

"Well, all right, Papa. I know you need to go to work at the shop. But please tell Mama to come up as soon as she can."

The girl's wide eyes showed her anxiety and confusion. She clearly knew that something was wrong, but she did not understand. The loss of Reuben was one thing, but this was different. She was like another person. Although her physical symptoms had disappeared, she had no desire to get up from her pallet. She had no desire to do anything but lie there. When her mother returned, she didn't care about talking with her, but just wanted her there. A fear of being alone had come over her. Something else was happening. She also had a fear of being closed in her room.

She wondered how this could be. She had always loved coming to her room to dream about her future with Reuben or to escape the teasing of her brother. Her room was her sanctuary, a place where her own thoughts could shut out the rest of the world. It was a place where she talked to God. Now what had happened to him? He seemed so far away. Was he even real?

Willing herself to get up and out of the closed-in cubicle, she arose to her feet and started out of the room, forgetting that Esther was sitting on the floor beside the pallet.

"Are you getting up for the day?" her mother asked hopefully. "You must be feeling much better."

"Oh, Mama,...yes...I don't know. I just know that I want to get out of here," Miriam said almost angrily.

"Out of here?" gasped Esther, stupefied.

"Yes! I need to get out!"

"But a few moments ago you wanted to lie down and have someone with you. What has happened?"

"I don't know what has happened!" her voice began rising. "I just know I want to get out!"

"But your hair, and your tunic. You are quite disheveled, my dear. Would you like for me to braid your hair and help you arrange your tunic?"

"Who cares about my hair or my tunic? No one but you will see me. And I surely don't care!" she shouted.

Esther could not adjust her thinking to this new aspect of her daughter. She was usually perfectly groomed and considered it improper to be otherwise. And she never shouted. Esther decided to let matters alone for a moment, as it was clear that something was definitely wrong with Miriam.

Miriam ran downstairs and immediately out into the courtyard, not turning to speak to Nathan or Jacob. She sank down on a cushion and stared into space, unmindful of anything about her. Nathan started to speak to her from the dining room, but Esther laid her hand on his arm and motioned him to silence. She drew him into the kitchen, putting her arms around his waist and her head on his chest.

"Oh, Nathan...something is terribly wrong with Miriam!" She sobbed quietly, her voice in a whisper. She is acting strangely. She wanted to get out of her room and cared nothing about her appearance—not even her hair! That's not like her at all."

Nathan held his wife close to him and stroked her hair, looking out the open doorway at his daughter sitting straight and still on the cushion.

"No, it isn't, my love. She was weeping when we were in her room. Could this all be because of Reuben? A short time ago she seemed to be her happy old self, and she had not been seeing Reuben. Or had she? Do you suppose, Esther, that they met somehow? David mentioned that Reuben seemed better also, but that he was downcast again. Perhaps if we leave her alone today, she'll be better tonight."

"Maybe I can interest her in doing some weaving. She always seems to enjoy that. I won't push her about her chores, though I'll be hard put myself to get everything done. But some things can wait. They will have to," she said resignedly with a sigh. "Now you must eat and get to the shop. You can ill afford to lose business."

Nathan and Jacob ate and left for the shop after Nathan told Esther he would send Jacob home around noon to check up on the situation. He stopped also to plant a kiss on Miriam's cheek, and the girl smiled wanly at him, turning once more to stare at the courtyard wall.

Back in Jericho David and Johhebed and family had arisen early to check on Saul and Samson, grease the axles, and get a prompt start home. Johhebed and Rhoda also wanted to choose some of the materials they had seen in the marketplace. These were so difficult to find in their region of Galilee, especially for the prices at which they were being offered. Johhebed knew she could strike a good bargain with the merchant, as the town was not full of travelers looking for wares.

After cleansing themselves and putting on fresh raiment, they warily looked at some of the food the innkeeper's wife had spread out on a low table in one corner of the inn. Some of it did not look very appetizing, in fact it did not at all look or smell fresh. They knew the bread had been baked that morning, and the fruit looked recently picked. The large figs particularly delighted them, and David decided to have some of the salted fish and cheese. He needed something substantial to provide strength for the journey home. The food they had brought with them was all gone, thanks to the hungry dogs along the way. David purchased extra fish, bread and figs to take with them.

"Is there somewhere we could pick some olives?" asked Rhoda, rather boldly, and Johhebed put her hand over the child's mouth in embarrassment.

"Yes, little one," said the round-faced, husky woman, smiling. We have plenty of trees out back and your brother can help you pick them. You must not live near here," she said turning to Johhebed.

"That's right," answered Johhebed. "We live in Cana of Galilee."

"Then take an extra supply. It's a long way from here, and olives are good food. We take pride in those grown around here."

Reuben was surprised at the geniality of this woman who was such a tigress during the night. Perhaps both of these qualities were needed in running such a business.

The stable keeper reported an unfortunate incident with Samson during the night, stating that he had caused quite a commotion trying to get to an Arabian mare. He was promptly tied up more securely, but continued to bray the rest of the night. David expressed his apologies for the bad manners of his beast and handed the man another coin for his trouble.

"You are a kind man," the stable keeper told him. "There should be more like you. I would venture to say you have been to hear the man, John the Baptist. You seem like someone who would be a follower of his."

"I have heard him twice," acknowledged David. "We plan to stop briefly to hear him again on our return journey. Shalom, my friend." David and Reuben led the donkeys to the nearby cart and proceeded to hitch them up, brushing away the swarms of flies which descended upon both men and animals.

Picking up Johhebed and Rhoda, they stopped first at the village well to refill the water jugs before retracing their route to the Jordan ford.

The current was fairly slow this time, but to be safe, David and Reuben got out and led the donkeys. They were on unfamiliar ground and their footing was not sure. Also, the cart was loaded heavier than when they left Cana. The crowd grew thicker as they came closer to the zor. A few Roman centurions were shouting, "Get over there!" "Make way!" "Move, Jewish pigs!"

Reuben's one desire was to find Jesus, and he took off quickly in the direction of John to see if he might find him.

There was much talk about the one whom John called the Lamb of God. The place reeked with people pressed close together: a combined odor of perspiration, garlic, stale food, and animal dung. It was unpleasant, but no one seemed to mind. All eyes were focused upon John, who preached relentlessly. But there was no sign of Jesus anywhere, and Reuben was clearly disappointed.

He wondered why he should care so much. He could always see him back at Nazareth when he went there. The urgency inside of him did not diminish with reason. After deciding that he had covered the entire territory to no avail, he searched for his family.

Meanwhile, he was hearing the words of John as they resounded over the area. He knew in his heart that he would never be the same again.

CHAPTER EIGHT

D avid would have little time to ponder on his journey after returning home. The chest needed to be
built for Jahdai of Garis, the carving had to be done,
and the early rains indicated that his wheat field must
be plowed and planted. Heavy dews had softened the
stony ground to some extent, and the time was right for
plowing. Reuben and Jonas could accomplish that, with
the assistance of the faithful Saul and Samson. Jonas
was especially good with a plow, for he never took his
eyes off of what he was doing. Reuben was more effec-
tive in the shop, but that could be worked out, David
contended. Jonas did need help.

Then there was the Day of Atonement coming up
when he would act as priest for his household. The
whole family must begin reflecting upon their sins.
Animals must be found by the men in Cana to offer as
sacrifices. David regretted not being able to journey to

Jerusalem for the holy day and hoped God would forgive him. Nathan too had hoped to go, but the plowing must be done immediately. They would worship in the synagogue.

David reflected on his desire that the family visit his brother and family in Capernaum and possibly effect a betrothal between Reuben and Deborah. However, that may have to wait until after the Feast of Tabernacles, which followed five days after the Day of Atonement. The feast day would hardly be a time of its usual joy for the family this year, considering Reuben's broken betrothal. If only the boy would come out of his despondency, David brooded.

Johhebed and Rhoda were let off at the house first, and they carried in the family clothing, along with the exciting new materials purchased in Jericho. The men then went on to the shop and unloaded the wood and the camel hide for Nathan.

"See to the animals, Reuben," David requested after the wood was unloaded, "and I'll get things in order before going home for our evening meal. We made good progress on our return journey, so I can still accomplish something here. Saul and Samson need a good rubdown, a measure of grain and some water. They may have no manners," he said with a smile, "but they served us well this week." He gave each one a hearty pat on the neck and went back into the shop.

As the men of the village gathered together that evening, there was much curiosity and questioning about what transpired on the way to Jericho and back—especially concerning John the Baptist. Did they go to hear him? What did he say? What did Reuben think?

David related in a general way what he had seen and heard but was reluctant to describe the baptism of Jesus and the voice from the heavens. He knew none would believe him and would merely call him daft. Perhaps I am, he thought.

"John is still preaching the same message of repentance and seems to believe that the Messiah is already on earth, in fact, here in the area of Palestine," David reported. "Crowds are coming to hear John, and numbers are being baptized in the waters of the Jordan. The interesting part is that they are coming from all walks of life—publicans, centurions, beggars, prostitutes, Pharisees, fishermen—and they listen. Many choose to follow him as disciples. Reuben seemed deeply touched but has said very little."

Nathan was silent and for once did not reproach his friend. In fact, he had little to say all evening, as if he were troubled about something.

"I brought you some camel hide," David informed him later as the group was beginning to disperse. "I'll bring it to your shop in the morning."

"I appreciate that," Nathan said soberly. "But I will pick it up."

"Is something the matter, Nathan?" David asked when they were alone. "You do not seem yourself."

"I have to be honest," replied Nathan, swallowing hard. "Miriam is not well. But we're not telling anyone yet, so please don't betray my confidence."

"Of course, I won't," assured David softly, looking his friend in the eyes. "But what is the nature of her illness?"

"I wish I really knew," sighed Nathan. "It is as though she were possessed at times. Then at other times she is fairly calm. She speaks very little to us."

"I am so sorry," David replied as he placed a hand on Nathan's shoulder. "Is there anything at all we can do? You know how willing we are to help you at all times."

"Yes, I know," replied Nathan sadly, "but in this case, I know of nothing at all anyone can do. We continue to look for a suitable husband for her and believe this might help a great deal. If only…"

Tears filled his eyes and he stopped, said Shalom and turned to go home, leaving David wondering what he was about to say, and also wondering about Miriam. Reuben must not be told about this, for it would be too grievous for him. The less said about Miriam, the better.

How sad, thought David, that the lives of these two young people are being affected this way. He felt certain that Miriam was suffering from despondency and that it had gone into a depression of the mind. Reuben is heartsick too, and that is why an alliance with Deborah must be made as soon as possible. He wondered if Nathan felt any guilt about the situation. Knowing Nathan, he would probably never say. He is as stubborn as an irksome camel!

The following morning, David and Reuben got an early start for the shop. A light but steady rain was falling which felt like a healing balm from the extreme heat they had been through. They looked forward to cutting out and fitting the pieces of the chest together. They had already drawn the plans, so it would merely be a matter of measuring, cutting and sanding down to a good finish. The chest would not be large so it would not take too long to accomplish this part. The rest would be more time consuming: the carving, assembling, the rubbing with oil. Of course, they would line the inside with cedar. David must choose the proper pieces of oak to enhance the beauty of the grain of the wood, but he was expert at that. Reuben would cut, sand and make the lining. He is a great help to me, reflected David.

Back at the house, Johhebed bemoaned the rain for one reason—her washing. She had trained Rhoda to do most of this for her on a regular basis, but today it would take them both to wash everything from their journey.

"Maybe it's only a shower, Rhoda," said Johhebed to her daughter, who openly dreaded the task ahead of them. "If so, we can lay out the clothing on the roof after it dries off. If the rain continues, however, we must dry it inside."

"If we have to do that," Rhoda complained, "there will be clothes everywhere and nothing to wear. We have nothing else clean to put on."

"I know, dear, but we have to make the best of it. The rain is needed, and it is certainly cooling things off. Now let's get to our job and trust that we'll have clean clothes tomorrow."

The sun did come out later in the day, and the air had a fresh, clean smell. By the time the men returned home, most of the clothing was dry and the meal was being set out on the table. Johhebed was grateful to be home and in familiar surroundings again. She even hummed a tune to her beloved flowers.

After the evening meal was over and David had returned from his usual meeting with the men of the town, the family gathered on the roof for worship. Reuben was restless and kept glancing in the direction of Miriam's house, as if he might steal a glimpse of her.

David cleared his throat to get his attention and indicated that he should sit on a cushion.

Raising his eyes heavenward, David began quoting the familiar words of the psalmist, "Thou, O God, did send a plentiful rain, whereby thou confirmed thy inheritance, when it was weary."

He then unrolled his scroll and read from the words of Moses concerning the forthcoming Day of Atonement, finishing with a prayer that God reveal to each of them their sins so that they might ask forgiveness on that holy day.

The family, weary from travel and the extra work of the day, started to leave the roof and seek rest from a good night's sleep. But David asked them to tarry a few moments. Even Johhebed didn't know what he wished to convey to them. She, Reuben, and Rhoda sank down heavily on the cushions once more and waited for David to speak. Reuben grimaced in annoyance, but said nothing.

"As you know," David said jovially, "the Feast of Tabernacles comes five days after the Day of Atonement. I have been thinking that since I can't go to Jerusalem, it would add to the joy of the occasion if we went to Capernaum and visited Azariah, Rachel and Deborah at that time. It's a week-long time of celebration, as you know, and I would love to see my family again. Their visit here was rather short and possibly ill-timed."

"But, what about the work at the shop, Father? Would you like me to stay and keep it open?" Reuben questioned hopefully.

"No, Reuben, that will not be necessary," David answered, not revealing that he was the main reason for their going. "The chest will be completed before then, the plowing should be done, and there is little else to concern me until we return. Others will be celebrating at the same time, so no one will expect work that week. It's an ideal time for us to go.

"Incidentally, I spoke with two men from Capernaum while we were listening to John—I wish now I could remember their names—and both are disciples of his and stay with him a good bit of the time. It made me think that perhaps Nathanael might like to ride along with us—probably on one of the family donkeys—and journey on to Bethsaida to visit his friend, Philip, who also follows John."

Reuben brightened somewhat at this, for it would give him the company of his friend on the way. There was no escaping the trip. He could count on that.

"I'll ask him tomorrow," said Reuben. "That is, if you're sure you don't wish me to keep the shop open."

"The shop will be closed. Ask him, son. Now, let's all get some much-needed rest and sleep," he said, looking at the three members of his family and smiling. He felt inwardly relieved that the possibility of a betrothal between Reuben and Deborah might be imminent. He could sleep well tonight.

But Reuben was low in spirit. His experience in the zor of Jordan seemed so far away now. He sensed in his heart his father's real reason for wanting to go to Capernaum. Deborah had as much as told him when she was in Cana. Although he was aware that she was somewhat attracted to him, he could tell that she was filled with compassion at his situation concerning Miriam. She would make some man a good wife, but he vowed it would not be him.

"Oh, Miriam," he later whispered as he lay on his pallet. "Do you still care for me as much as I care for you? I know in my heart that you do, and my arms ache to hold you." He closed his eyes and tried to imagine that her lips were on his...soft, sweet and responding. There was an emptiness and loneliness which he could not overcome. He wanted to tell her about his cousin, Jesus. Some day he must.

The Day of Atonement, ushered in ten days previously by the Feast of Trumpets, was a solemn occasion for the Jewish people. Moses had pronounced them both holy days—commanded by God—and they were to be observed in all humility and soul searching. It was desired that all Jewish men travel to Jerusalem for the Day of Atonement ceremony performed by the high priests, but the distance was too great for some when it would affect their livelihood and the feeding of their families. In such cases, services were held in the various synagogues, and the married men would act as priests for members of their families. The high priests in Jerusalem interceded for all Israelites.

The Day of Atonement was the only day in the year that any person entered the holy of holies in the temple. This would be the high priest. He must first bring a sin offering for himself and his family, remove his priestly garments, wash his body, and clothe himself in a simple garment of white linen representing purity and holiness. The people would watch for his return in agonizing repentance, for only when they saw him come out did they have the assurance of God's forgiveness.

"Tell us again about the goats, Papa," said Rhoda one evening before the holy days began.

"Well, before I tell you, you must promise not to become sad as you have done previously. I know how much you love animals, and you have always cried when I told you about the goats," David reminded her.

"I won't cry this time, Papa, really I won't."

"On the Day of Atonement, the high priest in Jerusalem brings two goats before the Lord and lots are cast to decide which one is to become the scapegoat. The other goat is killed as a sin offering, and its blood is sprinkled on the mercy seat of the ark of the covenant as an atonement for the sins of the people. The holy writ discloses that it is the blood which makes the atonement for our souls.

"The other goat, the scapegoat, signifies the removal of Israel's sin. The high priest places his hands on the head of the scapegoat and confesses all the iniquities of the nation Israel. The goat is then taken out to the wilderness and let go. This symbolizes the removal of the sins which have been confessed."

"But what if the goat comes back?"

"They never do, Rhoda. Perhaps God sees to it that it doesn't come back."

Tears began to well up in Rhoda's eyes, but she fought them back and then excused herself from the courtyard where they were sitting.

Few men in Cana were able to make the journey this year because of the early rains and the expediency of planting their crops. However, Nathanael decided to make the journey with his family, which meant he could not go to Capernaum with Reuben. He had hopes of meeting Philip afterward in the zor of the Jordan Valley in order to listen to John.

Nathan, David and Reuben joined others at the synagogue on both holy days. There various ones stood up to read the words of Moses and prayers from the sacred scrolls. Reuben found it difficult to concentrate on much of the services, as they were sitting close to Nathan and he was constantly reminded of his daughter. Reuben was thankful their eyes never met.

Four days after the Day of Atonement, David and his family departed for Capernaum. Saul and Samson showed their reluctance to begin the journey, but a smarting reminder from Reuben encouraged them to obediently plod forward under the direction of their masters and benefactors. They openly showed an affection for those who watered and fed them, but they preferred to move in their own timing.

The journey was accomplished by the ninth hour. The family had agreed to stay in an inn if it would inconvenience Azariah's household to stay with them. Pulling up in front of the whitewashed mud brick house, they were greeted by a view of the preparations being made for the Feast of Tabernacles. A tent-like structure was being erected beside the house, but no family member was in sight. David instructed the others to remain in the cart while he announced their arrival. He felt sure his sister-in-law would be home, and possibly Deborah.

"Shalom!" he shouted, reluctant to simply walk in uninvited.

A head popped over the low wall of the roof, and a bright smile broke over the joyful and surprised face of Rachel.

"David!" she called out, standing up and hurrying down the stairway. "What brings you here? Do come in and refresh yourself!"

Seeing the cart and the rest of the family, her eyes lit up and she rushed over to greet them, urging all to come inside. She fetched water and towels for their dusty hot faces and feet.

"We would like very much to celebrate the Feast of Tabernacles with you, if all is well with you," explained David, smiling warmly at Rachel. "We shall be happy to stay at an inn so as not to inconvenience you. We have given you no notice at all."

"You shall stay with us!" commanded Rachel. "Azaraiah, possibly with your help and Reuben's, can easily add to our tent. Come, Johhebed, let's plan the food for our feasting. Deborah is in the kitchen making sweet cakes now. Azariah will be home in about two hours, David. Why don't you lie down and rest awhile? Reuben seems to be caring for the animals. He's a fine young man, isn't he?"

"We think so," agreed David. "He's a trifle withdrawn now, but we shall speak of that later."

Rhoda brought in the clothing they had brought with them, and Johhebed returned to the cart to get the basket of grapes and cheeses she had brought, along with four loaves of freshly-baked bread.

"We didn't wish to come empty-handed," she said simply, setting the food down on a low table. "It's so good to see you, Rachel. And you too, Deborah," she said, smiling warmly and stopping to embrace her niece.

Deborah, wiping her flour-covered hands on her tunic, returned the embrace and beamed radiantly at Johhebed.

"And it is good to see you, my aunt!" she exclaimed. "Please excuse my appearance, but you can see what I've been doing."

"You have never looked more lovely," declared Johhebed. "It's your face, your eyes, your general countenance."

"She has good reason," interrupted Rachel, as Deborah blushed and returned to her culinary efforts.

Johhebed assumed that the young woman was rejoicing because Reuben had come for a visit. Her hope now was that Reuben would respond in a like manner.

The afternoon went by quickly, with happy plans being made for the next several days. Reuben came in and greeted the family after watering and feeding Saul and Samson and tying them up with his uncle's donkeys in the stable back of the house. There was pandemonium at first when the four animals met together, but when Eli and Enoch were satisfied that Saul and Samson would have their own food and would not encroach upon their rights, they calmed down and maintained a wary and watchful silence.

David decided to meet his brother on his way home. The happy reunion took place as the brothers embraced on the dusty streets in Capernaum, where parched and thirsty earth and shrubs cried out for refreshing rain.

Azariah was walking with a blustery fisherman of large proportions whom he introduced as Simon bar Jonas. The rough, bearded man smelled of the sea and grinned infectiously as he acknowledged the introduction.

"This is a pleasant surprise, David," asserted Azariah. "What brings you to Capernaum? How long can you stay?"

David explained the family's desire to celebrate the Feast of Tabernacles with them, but decided to wait until they were alone to discuss the betrothal contract.

"That is wonderful!" exclaimed Azariah. "I look forward to seeing the rest of the family also."

Then turning to Simon, he said, "We part here. Go in peace, Simon, and wish your mother-in-law well for me. It's always good to see you in Capernaum."

As the fisherman turned down a shady lane, bending under the weight of a wet net that was obviously in need of repair, David started to broach the subject of the betrothal. But something stopped him. Somehow, the timing was not right—or did he have a premonition that something was wrong? He could not tell, but he suddenly didn't feel right about it.

The two brothers spoke briefly about David's journey to Jericho. Azariah shared something of his day at the pottery shop. One of the jugs he was making came out imperfect and he had to completely remold it.

"My apprentice, Eleazar, is a wonderful help to me," he confided. "He's becoming like a son to me...a son I never had."

Soon they were home, and Azariah was greeting Johhebed, Rhoda and Reuben. As the evening progressed and the meal and worship service were over, David once more had the feeling that something was amiss. He briefly mentioned the betrothal between Deborah and Reuben, but the subject was changed, and he noticed Rachel and Azariah exchanging glances.

"We need to enlarge our tent a bit," suggested Azariah, and the talk immediately centered upon that subject. Reuben had gone to the stable temporarily and Deborah was busily engaged in washing up the dishes. David tried to broach the betrothal matter, but then Reuben returned and the subject could not be mentioned again that night.

David was confused and frustrated. He hoped the timing would be better tomorrow.

The family rose early the following morning, with David eager to broach the subject of the betrothal. Azariah had a bowl and three lamps to fire in the oven at his shop, so he invited David to accompany him and he eagerly accepted. This will be the perfect time to talk, reflected David.

Reuben was given the task of enlarging one end of the tent, so that it would accommodate two families comfortably. The women all busied themselves with baking and accomplishing the routine chores of sweeping, washing and tidying up the house.

Deborah and Rhoda went to the well for water while Johhebed and Rachel caught up on family news. Johhebed restrained her impulse to speak of the hoped-for betrothal, leaving the matter to David. But she was bursting to bring up the subject, aching inwardly for the well-being of her son. Just a little hint surely won't hurt, she told herself.

"We're ready now to consider Reuben's future," she remarked offhandedly. "Enough time has gone by to enable his heart to heal."

"Don't be too sure," Rachel evaded. "It took a whole year for Deborah."

Johhebed anticipated more encouragement than this from Rachel, and her face fell. Seeing this, Rachel laid her hand on Johhebed's arm and looked her kindly in the eyes.

"Now she is making us happy again. Perhaps she should have the privilege of telling you about it when she returns from the well."

Things were not going right, thought Johhebed, tightening her mouth and lowering her head as she feverishly kneaded the dough. She was confused but still hung on to the hope that the news somehow concerned Reuben. *That's it!* she reasoned. *Deborah has indicated to her parents a preference for Reuben. That's why she had such a glow after our arrival yesterday!*

Meanwhile, Azariah and David arrived at the shop, and a tall, muscular young man of about nineteen or twenty years greeted them with a flashing smile.

"David, this is my apprentice, Eleazar, that I spoke to you about. Eleazar, this is my brother, David."

"I have heard much of you, sir," acknowledged the young man warmly. "I believe you live in Cana?"

"Yes, I do. We're here to celebrate the Feast of Tabernacles with Azariah and the family. You must meet our son, Reuben. He's about your age—possibly a bit younger."

"I expect I shall when I come by to speak with Deborah. Did you tell your brother the news, Azariah?" he asked, turning to his employer.

"Well, no, not yet, but I was getting ready to." His eyes evaded David's inquisitive ones, as he nervously picked up some sticks of wood to add to the already hot oven.

"What news, my brother?" inquired David, his eyes narrowing and his head tilting to one side.

"Deborah is betrothed to Eleazar," Azariah answered simply, turning to face his brother.

David paled and momentarily lost his usual capacity for words, staring at Azariah in disbelief.

Eleazar sensed the tension and occupied himself by putting the clay vessels in the oven to be fired. He frowned at the reaction of his future father-in-law's brother—*my future uncle*—at the happy news. *What cloud has descended to mar our complete happiness?*

He avowed that nothing must disrupt his newfound joy.

"What's the matter, David?" inquired Azariah softly as he searched his brother's face. "Rachel and I are overjoyed at the turn of events. Come outside, and we will talk," he added, grasping David's arm and leading him out of the shop to a shady spot near by. "We need to be alone."

"But, I thought…," muttered David, his brow wrinkled and eyes questioning.

"I know what you thought…and I had hoped for the same thing," declared Azariah gently, placing his hand once more on his brother's arm. "But fate has changed the direction of our plans. Deborah and Eleazar—he came here recently from Tiberius to work with me—have fallen hopelessly in love. His parents died of a plague, and his two brothers were married and decided to continue as fishermen. I needed someone, and the word reached him by way of the sons of Zebedee—also fishermen. It was a streak of good fortune for me, for he is an excellent workman. He is also devout and of strong character. As I told you, he has become like a son to me—and he soon will be my son."

Azariah paused for a moment, wiped his brow with the back of his hand, and continued. "Our three daughters could not fill the place of a son, as you well know. We seldom see the married ones, as their lives are well taken up with their husbands' families. At least we have the house we began for Deborah and Caleb. Eleazar himself hopes to complete that."

"It's good things have worked out well for you," said David, taking a deep breath and regaining his composure but lacking the joy of his words.

A lump formed in his throat and seemed to work its way down into his stomach as he thought of Reuben and the emptiness that lay ahead of him. But he must not let on right now at the time of his brother's rejoicing.

Sensing David's disappointment, Azariah went to the shop doorway, stuck his head inside and told Eleazar he and David would be going home for awhile and would return later in the day to check the pieces of pottery being fired. He would appreciate his keeping the fire going for him.

Once at home, the men were met by a distressed Rachel and Deborah. "Johhebed is feeling ill and is lying down," said Rachel. Rhoda and Reuben are working on the tent. Would you please see to Johhebed, David?" she implored.

"Even Mama's good humor failed to help," Deborah added. "I'm afraid the whole matter is my fault, because I'm betrothed to Eleazar," she cried. "I so hope that you and Aunt Johhebed aren't angry with me," she beseeched. "Love is not always a matter of choice. It creeps upon us when least expected. Eleazar is my whole life now. Besides, you know where Reuben's heart is. It is certainly not with me.

Back in Cana, Miriam continued to be the cause of much grief to her family. She vacillated between wanting to be alone and desiring someone with her constantly. Nothing interested her—not even her weaving—and she went through her work mechanically, not engaging in her usual chatter or laughter with her mother. Except for Esther's purposeful singing and occasional remarks to Miriam, the house was void of human voices during the day. Birds sang outside, donkeys brayed, neighbors called one to another, but the household of Nathan was unusually silent until he and Jacob returned home from work.

"I cannot endure this much longer," confided Esther to Nathan one evening as they sat on the roof after Miriam and Jacob had retired early. "I cannot sit by and see our beloved daughter be destroyed by some evil spirit. That's what it seems is happening to her."

"Nor I," replied Nathan, staring ahead at nothing in particular. "But, what can we do? We know no one to seek out for a betrothal. And no one has come to us. The handsome gentile down the road obviously admires her, but heathens are out of the question! I would rather she would die unwed!"

"I have an answer, Nathan, but you will not approve," she sighed.

He waited a moment before answering.

"You are speaking of Reuben," he said simply. "You do not know how much I have agonized over that," he added, his voice rising. "I have searched my soul—especially just before the Day of Atonement. I want to do right by Mim and by God. The rabbi encouraged me to break the betrothal. Now Reuben has gone to hear John the Baptist. David told us this when he returned from their journey."

He bowed his head and covered his face with his hands, resting his elbows on his knees. Esther remained silent, not wishing to interrupt his thoughts. Minutes passed, and finally he raised his head.

"I don't know what to do," he whispered desperately. "But I too cannot stand by and watch Mim

become old before her time—and bewitched at that!"
His voice was hoarse and his eyes gleamed fiercely.

"Then you would consider…" She did not know
how to finish. It was Nathan who made the decisions in
the family. I must remember that, she thought.

"I will tell her in the morning, but God help my soul
if I am wrong!"

Love for her husband flooded Esther and she
reached over and squeezed his hand warmly. Her eyes
sparkled with genuine relief and admiration. Suddenly
she sobered.

"But what if Reuben has changed his mind?" she
panicked.

"Then there is nothing we can do. We will have to
accept that. Come, let us get our sleep. It's way past
time."

Arising at the usual hour after a night of very little
rest, Esther slipped downstairs quietly and went out to
light the fire to warm up the oven. Before going into the
kitchen to make up dough, she raised her face to the
sky and saw the first light of dawn in the east and the
faint light of a star in the darkness above. Smoke from
nearby fires was curling upwards, and the soft cooing of
a mourning dove broke the silence.

Could Nathan have had a repentant heart on the
Day of Atonement? Is he sorry he broke the betrothal
between Miriam and Reuben? No, she considered.
He is simply afraid of what might become of her. He
sees her as a very ill person and he loves her deeply.
Please let it work for them God, she earnestly prayed.

She busied herself in the kitchen, anxious that both
Miriam and Nathan would come downstairs. Out of the
corner of one eye she saw her daughter plod slowly

down the steps and enter the kitchen. She turned and embraced her, but felt no returning gesture. The girl's face was like a mask—unmoving and without expression. Esther winced and returned to her work, handing Miriam a bowl to set on the table.

"It's time for your father to come down," announced Esther. Receiving no answer, she went out to check the baking bread.

Then he came slowly, soberly and averting his eyes at first from his daughter. This will be hard to do, he thought to himself, but I must do it for the girl's sake. I cannot watch her in this condition any longer. She had long forsaken her appearance and looked ten years older. Her face was drawn and pale, her hair was stringy, and her hands shook. Her eyes held a glassy stare. He decided that now was the time.

"Mim," he faltered, "come out to the courtyard with me for a moment. I have something to tell you."

Miriam stared at him stonily and turned toward the open door. Going outside, she stopped and looked at him, waiting for what he had to say. It is of no consequence, she thought. What could he have to say that is important anyway?

"Sit down over here," he said, pointing at a faded yellow cushion and sitting down on another cushion facing her. Then he took hold of her hand and looked her in the eyes, stroking his beard with his other hand.

"Mim, your mother and I have come to an important decision. This isn't easy for me to say, and I want you to know that I am only saying it because we love you very much."

"What are you trying to tell me?" she asked in a flat voice.

"I think…we feel…I have reconsidered my stand on your betrothal to Reuben. He is in Capernaum now, and other plans might have been made for him. But if our two families can come to an agreement again, we are willing to enter into another betrothal contract between the two of you, that is if you still desire it to be so."

"It's too late, Papa. Reuben will marry his cousin in Capernaum. Word gets around, and I go to the well sometimes when others are there. I do not speak with them, but I hear them speak. I know he is in Capernaum now. Why else would he go? It really doesn't matter anyway."

Nathan squeezed her fingers tightly and looked at her compassionately.

"We will know in a few days, Mim. Meanwhile, we're telling you out of our love for you. I still feel uneasy about it all, but your happiness means a great deal to your mother and me. Whatever does happen, Mim, let's try to accept it and go on with our lives. We simply are trying to tell you in a very real way that we love you very much."

CHAPTER NINE

Reuben and his family returned to Cana the day after the Sabbath. Except for the joy of the two families at being together, the trip was disappointing. Deborah's unexpected betrothal dampened the hopes of David and Johhebed, and Johhebed had taken to her bed for two days. Reuben, however, felt the mantle of strain fall from his shoulders. Although he experienced no real happiness, he was filled with relief. It was difficult for him to watch Deborah and Eleazar gaze lovingly and unashamedly at each other, for it only intensified his desire for Miriam.

"Why won't her father relent?" he complained angrily to Deborah one day when they found themselves alone together. "You surely must have some idea how I feel, Deborah. She is my whole life!"

"I do know, Reuben," she confided. "I'm so very thankful for both you and me that Eleazar came into

157

my life, for I know what our parents were planning for awhile. You are a fine person...don't misunderstand me...but we both know it wouldn't have been good. I was attracted to you at first, but I soon realized how much you still love Miriam. Now I can only grieve for you."

"I grieve, too, but what can be done? Miriam's father is a stubborn donkey. He simply refuses to listen to me."

Now Reuben was home and more depressed than ever. What can I do? Where can I go? he asked himself. I cannot bear to live so close to Miriam and know that she is lost to me forever.

He was sitting in the courtyard just after the evening meal feeling angry and lost when he heard Nathan just outside the gate calling for David. Jumping up from his cushion, he went to the gate and bid Nathan come in. His heart pounded with emotion akin to hatred, but he maintained his calm out of respect.

"I'll go find father," he said. "He's preparing to go to meet the others. I'm sure he'll want to walk with you." And he turned and entered the house.

"I want to see you too, Reuben," Nathan shouted. "I have something to say to both of you."

Reuben froze for a moment. What more could Nathan possibly want of me? he thought resentfully. Hasn't he done enough to me already? His heart continued to beat hard in his chest as he stepped inside the door to call his father. David was already descending the stairs and was perplexed at the grim look on Reuben's face.

"What is it, son?" he questioned. "You look disturbed."

"It is Nathan. He's outside and wishes to see both of us—for what, I do not know. I'd rather not…"

"Of course you will," David interrupted. "Nathan is still our friend, you know."

Then David paled, thinking that Miriam's illness might have taken a turn for the worse. He put an arm around Reuben, and both went out to join Nathan by the wall where he was standing.

His head was bowed, but he looked up quickly as he heard the footsteps of the others. "Greetings, David," he said with a hint of a smile. "I hope you had a pleasant journey to Capernaum to see your brother." *Perhaps he will convey the message I want to hear before I say anything about my decision to him,* he thought hopefully. *If a betrothal has been effected with the girl Deborah, there will be no use my upsetting the situation further.*

"We had a fine visit except for Johhebed being slightly indisposed for two days."

"Why don't you tell him the reason, Father," suggested Reuben, who had been standing solemnly by. "As you say, we are all friends."

David shot Reuben a swift glance before giving Nathan an explanation.

"As I confided in you once, Nathan, we had hoped for a betrothal between Reuben and Deborah. But such was not to be. Deborah is completely taken by Azariah's apprentice, Eleazar, and they are betrothed and expecting to be married in the near future. Johhebed was quite shocked and took to her bed."

What is wrong with this world? thought Reuben. *Why do our parents manipulate our lives so? Everything was fine until Nathan ruined everything. Nothing he* can say today can be worse than what he has already done. His eyes challenged Nathan as he awaited what he had to say.

"May I sit down?" asked Nathan, clearing his throat and looking around for a cushion.

"Of course, my friend," offered David hospitably, pointing to a group of bright red cushions nearby. "Let's all sit down here."

Reuben dropped down reluctantly after the older men had been seated and continued to eye Nathan suspiciously.

Nathan bowed his head prayerfully for a moment and then looked first at Reuben, then at David.

"I have come on a difficult mission, difficult for me, that is. But I am feeling somewhat relieved now that I know that the betrothal between Reuben and Deborah did not take place."

David looked at his son and then fastened his gaze upon Nathan. Reuben's jaw fell, leaving him open-mouthed and astounded. David cocked his head to one side and frowned in disbelief.

"Whatever do you mean?" David asked. "I thought...that is...you...Please explain yourself, Nathan."

"Of course. You are due an explanation. That's precisely why I am here. Miriam has been ill...very ill. I mentioned it to you, David, but asked that you tell no one."

"Ill!" shouted Reuben. "Why could you not have told me, Father?"

"Quiet, son," David prompted. "I made a promise. Now let Nathan continue."

Reuben frowned with alarm and leaned forward to hear every word Nathan was saying.

"It has not been a physical illness, Reuben," explained Nathan, swallowing hard and tracing a pattern in the hard clay floor. Looking the young man in the eye, he continued. "It has been in the mind—a kind of deep depression. Her behavior has been strange, and she seldom speaks to us. She has withdrawn into herself, and we fear for her sanity. I realize now that it all began when I broke the betrothal between you two. I still feel I was right, but I love her too much to see her destroyed."

"Are you trying to tell us something further?" interrupted David, brushing away an unwelcome bee.

"Yes, my friend, " Nathan's voice broke and looked down for a moment. "If it is in your heart to agree, I am willing to renew the betrothal contract. I can stand no more to watch my daughter waste away. I am convinced that this is all she needs to bring her back to normal."

Reuben's eyes lit up, and a radiance spread over his entire countenance. He jumped up, unable to contain himself any longer. "When can I see her?" he asked excitedly. "This evening by the well? There is still time before sundown!"

"Hold on, Reuben," warned Nathan. "Miriam knows nothing about my being here. She does know that I planned to speak with you, but she was despondent, thinking that you had made other plans for your life. You would not like to see her the way she is now. I strongly suggest that you wait one more day at least. We are not even sure of her reaction."

David sat quietly, hardly believing what Nathan was saying, but feeling an intense surge of relief in his heart. Johhebed will rejoice, he said to himself. I will stay home tonight and tell her.

"Now, I must take my leave," said Nathan, slowly getting up from his cushion. The lines on his face revealed the toll Miriam's illness and his subsequent decision had taken.

This is not easy on him, sympathized David silently.

"I think I'll forego our usual meeting with the others," David informed Nathan. "I need to be with my family and resolve some problems which have weighed heavily on our hearts. Before you leave, Nathan, I want you to know my gratitude and my respect for you. You are putting others above yourself, and I realize how difficult this is for you in this instance. Your commitment to God is great and will continue to be. I'm very much aware of that."

David embraced his friend, and tears blurred his eyes. Reuben joined in the embrace and was likewise visibly moved. Despair gave way to ecstasy. He was deeply touched by his future father-in-law's action. It was as if he had been given new life and his whole being quivered expectantly. He could no longer despise Nathan. He was giving him too much—at a sacrifice of his own convictions.

While David and Reuben rushed into the kitchen to impart the news to Johhebed, Nathan wearily plodded homeward, also deciding to forego his usual meeting with his friends. He was emotionally spent but experienced a certain relief in having done this thing. The misgivings remained, but he accepted the fact that he had acted wisely for the sake of his family.

"Esther! Mim!" he called as he entered the gate to his home and sank down on one of the faded yellow cushions in the courtyard.

"What is it, Nathan?" inquired Esther, the first to appear.

"Wait until Mim comes," he said. "It's important that she be here."

"You mean…," Esther stammered. "Did you go to see David and Reuben?"

"I said wait," he commanded firmly. "I will tell you both at once."

Esther could not tell by his countenance whether the news was good or bad. *Nathan can be difficult sometimes,* she complained to herself. *He is so self-willed, in spite of the fact that he is a good man and a good husband.*

"Miriam! I'm waiting!" he called sharply, using her full name as he often did when upset.

Miriam shuffled in, her countenance stoic and her hair in disarray.

Nathan looked at her and once more felt compassion envelop him, dissipating his irritation.

"Mim, please sit down. I have news for you."

The slight smile showing in his upturned lips and his eyes made Esther's heart leap, but Miriam remained solemn.

"I have been to see David and Reuben, and Reuben is not betrothed to Deborah after all. She is making plans to marry another, and Reuben wished no alliance with her anyway. I have given my consent for you and Reuben to renew your betrothal if you so desire." His voice broke at the end and tears filled his eyes as he reached for Miriam's hand.

Esther let out a cry, but stifled it immediately. Miriam's response was of the utmost importance, and two anxious pairs of eyes fixed their gaze upon her expectantly, awaiting her reaction. It was slow, as the words of her father impressed themselves on her consciousness. Suddenly, her eyes widened and began to water and tears started to stream down her still rounded cheeks. With a burst of emotion, she moved closer to embrace her father and sobbed relentlessly as he held her close.

"Mim," he choked, "I hope these are tears of joy and not of sadness."

Releasing her hold upon him, she gazed softly into his eyes. "Sadness, Father? I have cried my tears of sadness for a long time. There can be no more sadness now! You have brought my life back to me! I love you, Father." She embraced him again.

Miriam heard a quiet sobbing behind her and turned to see her mother's face buried in her hands. The girl went quickly to her and stroked her bowed head.

"I know you've both been worried about me, but I'm going to be all right now. I just feel it. It's as if something very heavy has been removed from my whole body, and I see through different eyes. The past few weeks or months have been hazy. I don't even know what time of year it is or what has happened around me. I've lived in fear—but in fear of what, I don't know. Please forgive me for upsetting you. I knew you were troubled, but it didn't matter to me. I'm so sorry." She turned to her father. "When may I see Reuben? He does want to see me, doesn't he?"

"He wants very much to see you, Mim, but I suggest that you take stock of yourself before you meet him. Your mother can help you if necessary, but surely you realize how you have let yourself go." He scrutinized her through squinted eyes. "In fact, I shall see David in the morning and arrange for the family to come here for a meal tomorrow evening. We can effect the betrothal then if it meets with their approval. They are pleased about it, however, so I see no problem. I told Reuben I would have to await your reaction before you could meet."

Miriam put her hand to her hair and looked down at her clothing and bare feet with dismay. "Oh!" she exclaimed softly. "Look at me! Is this really me?" She picked up a fold of her tunic in disbelief. "I remember little about all of this except a deep sense of sorrow. Little else mattered. How can I ever make it up to you? I'll try and make it up to God on the Day of Atonement."

"The Day of Atonement is over, little one," said Nathan solemnly. "We tried to tell you about it but you did not listen. It was as if you were in another world." He looked up at the sky and back at Esther. "Now we must have our time of worship. God must not find us disobedient." He arose and walked over to the stairs leading to the roof.

Esther smiled at Miriam and followed her husband, motioning to Jacob who was standing in the doorway. Miriam wanted to rush immediately to her room and do something about her appearance, but decided to wait until after worship. New life was flowing back into her and she could feel the wellspring of hope filling her entire being.

Oh, Reuben, she thought warmly. I can hardly believe what is happening. We've been apart so long without any hope at all, and suddenly the bad dream is over. My love for you never failed, Reuben...only my strength and my will to live.

The family meeting was arranged for the following evening. Reuben could hardly contain himself and urged his father to close the shop early in honor of the occasion. David was willing to comply, being equally excited over the prospects.

Miriam awoke before sunrise, sleepily aware that something special was happening. She had slept little during the night, her heart beating fast with excitement and joy. What sleep she did get was from pure exhaustion. But now adrenalin charged her blood and provided an unusual and long overdue burst of energy.

The dawn of the new day shed enough light for her to take an empty jar to the well. Her first concern was to wash her hair thoroughly and comb it until there was not a tangle remaining. It must be *clean and shiny* tonight, she told herself. I wish I could wear it loose to please Reuben. Perhaps after we are betrothed again Mama and Papa will allow me to unbraid it. It is quite proper, but Mama always told me I was simply too young. Surely they will agree now.

Miriam found herself tiring easily as she went about her chores during the day. But with the lifting of her spirits she could laugh and converse with her mother again. Esther was wise enough to say little about it, but her face glowed with happiness as her daughter exhibited all signs of coming out of the terrible depression which had so tightly held her in its grasp.

"What do you plan to wear tonight, Miriam?" she asked while the two were laying out the clothes to dry in the bright sun.

"Reuben likes my pink tunic. I think I'll wear that one. At least it's clean as I haven't wanted to put it on for so long."

Up in her room later, Miriam took great care with dressing and arranging her hair. She took up a shiny piece of metal which she often used to see her reflection and was appalled at the dark circles under her eyes. I can do nothing about that, she observed, putting down the metal and descending the stairs to join the family. She had chosen her newest pair of sandals to wear. From one of the pots she picked a white blossom and placed it in her blue girdle. Once again she was ready to meet her beloved Reuben.

"I feel nervous," she confided to her mother as they prepared the meal together and looked for the others to come. What if Reuben or David have changed their minds?"

"Don't worry, my dear one," said Esther confidently. "From all I hear, Reuben seeks no other than you. This has been a difficult time for him also. Johhebed has been quite worried about him and that is why they sought another betrothal."

"Oh, there are so many what ifs, Mama, but I guess I mustn't think of them. Here come David and Johhebed now and..." She stopped short and gazed at the person so dear to her who was standing at the gate and smiling broadly. A lump formed in her throat and she tried to swallow it.

Decorum prevented them from running into each other's arms as they so desperately desired, but tears filled the eyes of both as their radiant faces greeted one another. The bad dream was over. With the exception of the formalities between their parents, their worlds had become one again.

"*Shalom*, Miriam," said Reuben touching her ever so lightly on the shoulder, sending tingles over her skin.

"*Shalom,* Reuben," greeted Miriam with a smile, all feelings of shyness and nervousness gone. Esther noticed the brightness of her eyes and the love which poured from them and knew Nathan had done the right thing. He will adjust somehow, she thought. We have our daughter back.

It was a simple matter for the two families to make the plans. Nathan wisely kept the conversation away from John the Baptist. Esther and Miriam feared he might bring up the unwelcome subject, but his restraint proved his real love for his daughter. Both families knew that he was hurting, but they could also see the relief on his face regarding Miriam. Nathan himself was depending upon the premise that God knew his heart and that he was in no way turning from him. Perhaps Reuben and Miriam will not follow the Baptist, he inwardly hoped.

Reuben and Miriam began seeing each other the following evening at their trysting place, the well. He was there waiting before she left her house and they ran to meet as soon as he saw her leave. The streets were empty, and they stopped by the first clump of oleander bushes to embrace. They could wait no longer.

"Oh, Miriam, my love!" he cried out softly. "You can never know what I have gone through without you. And you…, you have been ill, your father says. My poor darling." He touched her cheek gently. "I didn't know and did nothing for you."

"I felt like I was dying," confessed Miriam, "but I know now it was because you were gone from me and all my hope was also gone. Oh Reuben, I love you so. Please don't ever leave me!"

"I won't! I swear I won't! Ever!"

They walked to the well. There he put his finger under her chin and tipped up her face to his, placing his lips tenderly on hers and eagerly tasting their sweet response.

"When, Miriam? When can we be married? Surely we don't have to wait a year this time?" He ran his hands through her long shiny hair, which her mother had said she could leave unbraided.

"Papa says he agrees to our being married in two months since we have already been betrothed so long before. My wedding gown is almost completed, but of course I must ask my bridesmaids and make other plans. How about your cousins in Nazareth? Will you be able to invite them—and also your relatives in Capernaum?" She felt a small stab of jealousy concerning Deborah, although she knew she really had no reason to be jealous.

"Miriam, it's almost time for us to go now, but I want to tell you much about my cousin, Jesus, in Nazareth. I plan to go there one day soon and invite them all to the wedding. But I also want to go for another reason. I'll tell you more later. There's something strange about him. I can't put my finger on it. I really feel drawn to go over there again."

"I want to hear about it, Reuben, but now it's time for me to leave. It will be more difficult each day until we are wed and will not have to meet like this." Their arms entwined once more and they kissed briefly and almost fiercely. "Shalom, Reuben," and she was gone.

Reuben lingered until she was out of sight and wended his way homeward. The evening sky had never looked more beautiful to him.

In the next few days, Miriam began to blossom

more and more. She threw herself into her daily chores with a new burst of energy, and her mind was filled with dreams and plans. Even Jacob rejoiced over her change of heart and attitude. Now he was relieved of some of the extra chores he had been forced to do.

"I don't see how anyone can carry on so about getting married," he told his sister one day as she was singing while washing and drying the dishes after the evening meal. "You won't catch me being that foolish. No mere girl is worth all that!"

"Ha!" she countered. "You just wait until little Naomi down the street grows up. She's pretty now, but one day she'll be beautiful. You'll be begging Papa and Mama to let you be betrothed to her—if she'll have you." She flicked her drying towel at him as he awkwardly jumped out of the way.

"That's a lie, and you know it!" the rangy dark-haired boy all but shouted, turning on his heels and walking away.

A smile stole over Miriam's face, and she hastened to throw out the dishwater and get ready to meet Reuben. This would be her last night to see him for a couple of days, since he planned to leave in the morning for Nazareth.

Her heart quickened as she swiftly made her way to the well, arriving there the same time as Reuben. After a brief embrace and tender kiss, Reuben held her at arm's length as he told her of his plans, his eyes shining with excitement.

"Miriam, I want so much for you to meet my cousin, Jesus, as I told you. I'll invite him and his family to the wedding feast, of course. I pray he'll be there when I arrive tomorrow. You see," he continued, his voice softening, "there's something different about him which I can't explain. The last time I saw him was in the zor of the Jordan Valley when my family and I went to hear John the Baptist."

"Oh, Reuben, you did go! Does Papa know about it? If not…and if he finds out…he might change his mind again." Her eyes were wide with fright.

"He knows about it, my sweet. That's one thing I can't understand about him. Why he let us become betrothed again after he knew I had been to see John."

Reuben proceeded to quickly explain to Miriam about the baptism of Jesus, how John had called him the Lamb of God, whose way he was preparing, and how he and David had heard the voice from above.

"Miriam," he continued with knitted brows and rising excitement, "Father told me that Jesus was born in Bethlehem, just like the prophet Micah predicted about Messiah. And then Father went to the synagogue to look at the scrolls of Isaias."

"What did he find out?" she asked breathlessly.

"That Messiah would be born of a virgin. He had read that before, of course, but it took on new meaning after Mother confessed later—when asked about it— that her cousin Mary became with child out of wedlock, even though she said she knew no man. Jesus' father, Joseph, married her anyway as they were already betrothed. Mother was ashamed to talk about it, as it was a family scandal. But now…"

Miriam was blushing at the tone of the conversation, but she wanted to hear more and asked, "Now what, Reuben? Please go on!"

"Father asked her about Mary's marriage the other day and where Jesus was born." Reuben's eye's glistened as he continued. "When she told him about it, he shared with her what we had seen and heard at the baptism of Jesus. You see, Mother and Rhoda were sitting back in the shade at the time, and we knew they would consider us daft if we told them."

"Reuben! This is a serious thing you're implying. Do you think?..."

"I mean that I want to find out the truth, Miriam! I must go to Nazareth and find Jesus."

"Oh, yes, Rueben! I want to know, also. But I'm so afraid of Papa and what he will do. We mustn't let him know anything until...well, until..."

"We will not hide the truth, Miriam. Please don't fret about anything right now."

"I'll try hard. But now I must go, my dearest love. I'll be waiting anxiously for your return."

After a brief embrace, she turned and hurried home. Darkness was coming swiftly and she did not wish to anger her parents, especially now.

Miriam's mind was swimming in a torrent of thoughts. Reuben's startling revelation was almost too much for her to comprehend. Does he really believe a mere carpenter from Nazareth could be the Messiah? Couldn't all these things be just a coincidence—the virgin birth (if that were really so), Bethlehem, the forerunner John, the sound from heaven?

Reuben left his home at dawn the following morning. He had decided to ride Samson as the beloved beast needed exercise, and David and Jonas would not be using him for the next two or three days. Reuben was absorbed in thought when, in a turn in the road, he encountered Simon, a Zealot who lived in Cana but had been working feverishly with the extremist guerilla group to overthrow the Roman occupation. Reuben knew him but slightly, as their paths rarely crossed.

"Greetings, Simon! Where are you headed this time?" he asked as Samson caught up with the walking traveler.

The swarthy, fierce-eyed Simon flashed a smile of recognition at Reuben and replied, "I'm headed for Nazareth." His brown tunic, belted with leather, revealed a knife at the waistline. He carried nothing else with him. Muscular arms and legs indicated a physically active young man. He had the habit of looking warily over his shoulder and to one side or the other as if in constant danger. His right hand automatically touched the knife handle as he did so.

"So am I," answered Reuben, dismounting from Samson and falling in step with Simon while leading the donkey by the reins. "May I ask what takes you to Nazareth? Are the Romans causing trouble there?"

"Actually, no. We've heard of a man who has a new teaching. He's preaching in the synagogue and on the hillsides around there. Nazareth is his home, but he is speaking of a kingdom. I'm interested in finding out if he opposes Roman rule."

Reuben's senses quickened, and he eagerly asked, "Who is this man? What is his name?" Excitement rose within him as he awaited the answer.

"Jesus. That's about all I know about him except that he's a carpenter. I thought perhaps he might wish to join the Zealots...that is, if he feels as we do."

"Perhaps," said Reuben vaguely, all the while considering the words "kingdom" and "preaching" which Simon had uttered. The Jesus I know is no Zealot, Reuben pondered. He's not an aggressive person, not passive either, but obviously compassionate and compelling. It's difficult to describe him…to understand him. "Jesus is my cousin," he informed Simon. "I came to invite him to my wedding in about two months."

"So you know him," remarked Simon with interest. "Then you must know that our friend Nathanael recently became his follower. I saw his father yesterday and he told me about it."

"Nathanael?" gasped Reuben in surprise. "I knew he planned to see and hear John the Baptist after he went to Jerusalem, but that has been many weeks ago. I've been looking for him to return to Cana. How and where did he meet Jesus?"

"Near Jericho. His friend Philip brought him to Jesus. But it seems that Jesus knew his name before they met. A rather unusual circumstance. They are in Galilee now. And John the Baptist is in prison."

"In prison!" Reuben stopped short, causing Simon to inadvertently butt him in the arm. "Whatever for? Where?"

"Word has it that Herod had him put there because he criticized Herod for marrying Herodias, the former wife of Herod's brother. He's in that foul pest hole in the fortress of Machaerus. I personally never heard the man speak. Maybe he deserved it," Simon conjectured. "He did stir up people they say; but then who am I to be judgmental about that?" he chuckled.

The two young men conversed of more commonplace matters for awhile, stopping twice to refresh themselves in the cool trickle of a stream. Seasonal rains would soon swell these life-giving oases according to the regular order of the elements.

Reuben decided to stop and see Mary first before looking for Jesus, so he and Simon parted at the familiar whitewashed mud brick house. The noise of chickens clucking led him to walk to the small but neat yard at the rear. There he found Mary throwing crumbs of bread to a fluttering huddle of squawking hens.

"Shalom, cousin Mary!" he shouted to make himself heard.

Turning sharply, the lovely and youthful-looking matron paused in surprise, as a radiant smile brightened her face.

"Oh, Reuben—what a surprise!" she exclaimed, approaching him with outstretched arms. Embracing him, she added, "Please come inside. It's so good to see you. What brings you to our humble little town of Nazareth?"

"I came to invite you and your family to my wedding," he said with a grin. "Miriam and I...well, we are betrothed again, and we want you to join us. Mother asks if you will assist at the wedding feast the second new moon from now.

"We shall be honored to come," asserted Mary as they strolled inside. "And I will be happy indeed to serve in any capacity at the feast."

Discretion prevented her from pressing Reuben concerning the second change in plans. After Reuben washed his face, hands and feet, they chatted for awhile. Mary brought him bread, grapes and cold goat's milk, chilled by a nearby spring. One of her sons came in but had little to say to Reuben. He gulped down what food was left on the platter before a quick departure.

Mary lowered her eyes and softly murmured, "Forgive Noah's rudeness. He does not take after Jesus or his other brothers."

"Don't concern yourself, Cousin Mary. But tell me, how is Jesus, and where can I find him?"

A faraway look came on Mary's face and she said, "He is somewhere in the area, but I rarely know his whereabouts. He does much teaching in the synagogues around here and many people are following him. Some were disciples of John the Baptist, who is now in prison. You may have to ask around to find him." Her expression held a hint of sadness, as if her son was almost lost to her.

"I have heard...I need to know..." He stopped short as Mary looked him in the eyes soulfully. It was as if she were trying to tell him something she was forbidden to say.

"It is best that you seek Jesus out yourself, Reuben. Then you can evaluate what you have heard, or what you need to know."

CHAPTER TEN

Reuben stayed with Mary as long as courtesy allowed before proceeding to the synagogue. His heart sank as he found no one around, but he felt certain that someone in the town would know where Jesus had gone. The carpenter shop, that was it! The family still required his skills for a living. Mary had not mentioned that.

He found his way to the familiar location and noticed some children playing outside. He all but ran to the doorway but stopped short when he saw Jesus' brother James inside. The shop was untidy, and James was sitting on a bench laughing with another young man. Jesus was nowhere to be seen.

"Greetings," shouted James to Reuben, recognizing his cousin. "What brings you to Nazareth? Is business so bad that you have come here for customers?"

Reuben was aware of the rivalry between neighboring towns and took the remark in good humor. "Business is good, as a matter of fact, my cousin," he answered with a smile. "I've come to invite you to my wedding the first Wednesday after the second new moon. Miriam and I hope your whole family will come.

"That we shall," grinned James, "but don't count too much on Jesus. He's rarely home any more and has taken to preaching most of the time. If you ask me, he's a bit daft."

Reuben ignored the remark and casually asked, "Where is he preaching now?"

"He left a few hours ago for Capernaum. With so many people following him to hear him preach, he's probably standing on some hillside giving his 'words of wisdom,'" James sneered.

"I may try to catch up with him," said Reuben, "after I pick up my donkey at your house. I left him to rest awhile. Shalom. I'll look for you at the wedding feast."

"It will be a welcome relief from the boredom around here," answered James, wiping his face with a grimy rag.

Samson nudged Reuben as he took the reins from around a post near Mary's house. Reuben did not attempt to look for Mary, as he was anxious to catch up with Jesus. James certainly doesn't think of Jesus as anyone special, he thought, mounting the docile donkey. But Mary...she had a different reaction. I couldn't quite get what she was saying, but she is obviously affected by this son of hers.

The countryside was much like that around his hometown of Cana—barley and wheat fields, olive trees, and vineyards. The road wound around the hillsides, and Samson gave Reuben a rather rocky ride, paying little heed to where he was stepping. Reuben loved the beast but often wondered about his intelligence. Today he smelled even stronger than usual and kept switching his tail to ward off the swarms of flies landing on his body.

Around a horseshoe curve, a gathering of people materialized on a hillside. One white-robed figure stood out among all others. His face was hidden from Reuben, but the voice belonged to the person he so anxiously sought. Reuben's heart skipped a beat, and he hastened to dismount Samson, tie him up and join the listening crowd. He would stay in the background at first so as to be free to assess the situation without conversing with Jesus. However, it was apparent that Jesus took little heed of others as he spoke of the kingdom of heaven, of repentance, and of becoming as little children.

How can he speak with such authority? Reuben asked himself. He speaks as if he knows God personally, and he surely knows the Scriptures.

Looking around, Reuben saw Nathanael and Simon standing with another young man who must be Philip, Nathanael's friend. He decided to edge his way quietly around to where they stood, anxious to see Nathanael and learn exactly what drew him to Jesus enough to influence him to become a disciple. Nathanael had previously scoffed at Philip for following John the Baptist. He surely can tell me something, Reuben deduced.

"Greetings, my friend, " he said softly, touching Nathanael on the arm. "I certainly didn't expect to find you here. Is it true what I hear—that you are now following Jesus?"

"Reuben!" exclaimed Nathanael in a lowered tone as he turned and smiled to the see the owner of the familiar voice. "What a good surprise to meet you in such an unexpected place! Yes, Reuben, I am now a follower of the carpenter from Nazareth. I'll tell you more later. Let's listen to what he is saying."

An hour later, Reuben was still standing in the same spot, unaware of the heat of the day or of the people around him. He could hardly take in the wisdom of this simple carpenter cousin, and he could not for a moment question his authority. Where it came from, he could not be certain. But he was beginning to develop some strong convictions—difficult as they were to comprehend.

Soon Jesus stopped speaking to the crowd and bent down to take a little child in his arms. The child looked at him adoringly with wide brown eyes, and placed her arms around his neck. He patted her and gently put her down, speaking in soft tones to individuals who came up to him. Now is the time, thought Reuben, as he excused himself from his friends before going over to see his cousin.

"I'll be back shortly," he addressed Nathanael. "Please wait for me. I do need to talk with you, but now I must speak with Jesus for a moment before he journeys further."

"I'll be here," answered Nathanael, "although I plan to follow Jesus to Capernaum when he leaves. I'm anxious to speak with you also, Reuben. Make haste now, before he decides to depart."

Elbowing his way through the dispersing crowd, Reuben caught up to Jesus as he was turning to descend the hill in the company of two men.

"Jesus!" called Reuben. His cousin turned almost at the instant he called him. The two embraced, and

Reuben was introduced to two men by the names of Andrew and John who departed immediately and left Jesus and Reuben alone.

"I have come to invite you and your family to my wedding," he said, flustered at his inability to ask what was really on his mind. "Your mother knows the details concerning the date and the place of the wedding feast."

There is so much I want to say to him, but my tongue is tied, thought Reuben. What is it about this man that is so awesome? I simply must ask him one question.

"Before you leave, Jesus, please give me your opinion on one matter of utmost importance to me and to my betrothed, Miriam."

Jesus beckoned him to a spot void of people and sat down in a relaxed manner, motioning Reuben to do the same. Reuben's gaze locked with his, and once again he felt unexplainably drawn by those compassionate, all-knowing eyes. He was reminded of his first visit to the carpenter's shop in Nazareth. Again he was filled with the feeling that there was something special indeed about this man.

"I know you were baptized by John the Baptist," Reuben continued. "My family and I were there and saw you. I was reluctant to go that day, for my betrothal had just been broken because my father and mother were interested in the man and had decided to follow his teachings."

Reuben waited for a moment to see the reaction of Jesus. Receiving none, he continued. "I became impressed with his teachings myself that day. Although our betrothal contract has been renewed, I am concerned about the fact that Miriam's father believes God will punish us if we marry and follow any teaching other than that which was handed down by Moses and written in the law."

"Do you think God will punish you?" Jesus asked, continuing to look Reuben straight in the eyes.

"I...I...don't know. But I do know that we both love God and will continue to worship him."

"It is enough," said Jesus, and he rose to take his leave. Assuring Reuben that he would attend his wedding, he joined Andrew and John and started toward the road.

Reuben stood transfixed for a few moments and then remembered Nathanael. He would be leaving also, so he quickly joined his friend and took him aside.

"Nathanael," he spoke in a low voice. "Tell me what you know about Jesus. Even though he is my cousin, I feel I do not really know him. It's important that I know all you can tell me."

"I have little time now, Reuben, but I can only say that I am drawn to him as though God himself had placed me with him. I wish nothing but to follow him. It all happened suddenly. Philip had said to me, 'We have found him, of whom Moses in the law and the prophets wrote Jesus of Nazareth, the son of Joseph.' I jokingly, and a bit seriously too, said to Philip, 'Can any good thing come out of Nazareth?' and he told me to come and see.

"When we approached Jesus, he looked at me and said, 'Behold an Israelite indeed, in whom there is no dishonesty!' I asked him when he had ever known me, and he told me, 'Before Philip called you, when you were under the fig tree, I saw you.'

"Reuben, I honestly don't know how I happened to answer him like I did, but I believe my answer with all my heart now."

"What did you say to him?" asked Reuben excitedly.

"I said...I said, 'Rabbi, you are the son of God; you are the king of Israel.'"

Reuben paled and took hold of his friend's arm, beginning to tremble all over.

"You mean...you believe?..."

"Yes, Reuben, I believe that Jesus is our long-awaited Messiah. But there is more. Jesus answered me and said, 'Because I said to you that I saw you under the fig tree, you believe? You shall see greater things than these. Truly, truly, I say unto you, hereafter you shall see heaven open and the angels of God ascending and descending upon the Son of Man.' It's true, Reuben," Nathanael declared with feeling. "He said those things to me, and I believe him!"

Reuben was unable to answer Nathanael for a few moments. He was unable to comprehend what he had said to him and put it together with what Jesus had said and what he had seen and heard at the baptism of Jesus. It was almost too much for him to assimilate.

"I know it is difficult for you to understand all that I am saying, Reuben," assured Nathanael kindly, "but I know that I must follow Jesus and have known from the moment I met him. Nothing in life means as much to me now, and I sense in my heart that he was sent from God. I hope you too will come to feel as I do and know in your heart that he is Messiah."

"Perhaps I shall, but right now I need time," answered Reuben shakily. "There is Miriam to consider, of course. We are betrothed again, and I want very much for you to attend me at our wedding right after the second new moon from now."

"I shall be honored and will greatly look forward to it. I'm happy for you. Miriam is a beautiful and fine young woman. Now I must leave and join the others. Until then, shalom!"

The two young men embraced and turned to go their respective ways. Nathanael joined Philip and Simon, and Reuben returned to Samson to head back to Nazareth and Cana. His heart beat wildly as he contemplated the confrontation with Jesus and Nathanael, and his mind swam with the possibilities presented to him. He had come for the truth, and now he wondered if he had found it. Deep inside he felt that there was something very real about what he had seen and heard. Even Mary had deepened this conviction with her simple but subtle words and expressions.

I can hardly wait to tell Miriam and Father, he said to himself as he was jostled and bounced by Samson on the way home. He stopped twice to water the animal, but found it difficult to even keep his mind on that simple matter.

But the Messiah will be a king, he asserted to himself. Jesus is a mere carpenter and is doing nothing about the Roman rule and is not setting up his own kingdom. He does speak of the kingdom of heaven, but in simple and lowly terms. He has no form of government. I am very confused, he told himself, but I sense something real and true about it all.

It began to rain before he arrived back in Cana which soothed more than irritated him. He knew it was a blessing from God and somehow he felt very close to him at that time. It would be dark by the time he arrived home, and he would not see Miriam. He had actually not planned to see her until the next evening, not knowing what he would find in Nazareth. What he had found was overwhelming him to the exclusion of everything, save his love for Miriam. Nothing else mattered

Reuben arrived home during family worship and slipped quietly upstairs to the roof, sitting down on the nearest cushion. His father was reading from the familiar scroll of Isaias the words, "And the spirit of the Lord shall rest upon him, the spirit of wisdom and understanding, the spirit of counsel and might, the spirit of knowledge and of the fear of the Lord."

As David rocked back and forth while reading the words the family had heard since they were all children, Reuben sat pensively, drinking in every word. He was trying to relate these words to his cousin Jesus, and he could find no discrepancy. Excitement built inside him, and he wanted to stop everything and tell what he had heard and seen. He wanted especially to share these things with his father and watch for his reaction. David was well versed in the Scriptures—just like any devout Jew—but he was not impulsive. He would not jump to conclusions unduly.

Surely Father is praying longer than usual tonight, thought Reuben as his mind wandered from the holy petitions. Does he have to speak to God so much about our sinfulness? Then his mind reverted to the words he had heard spoken by Jesus, and he was ashamed. Jesus had pronounced the need for repentance, and of course John the Baptist had done the same. Reuben's mind was so full that he could not seem to think properly. He did need time and his father's opinion.

After embracing his mother and Rhoda and telling them of his brief visit with Mary, he waited for David to put away the sacred scroll and his prayer shawl in the container.

"How was your journey, my son?" asked David, putting an arm around Reuben. "Did you invite our cousins to the wedding?"

"Yes, Father. But so much happened—much more. I can hardly take it all in. Please let me tell you about it. I need to talk about it."

As the women left the roof, David and Reuben sat down facing each other. Reuben tried to relate every detail of his talk with Mary, his short talk with James, and even his encounter with Simon on the road. Then his voice rose as he told of finding Jesus preaching on the hillside just outside of Nazareth and of the things Nathanael told him. He particularly remembered the words of Jesus when speaking with him about his forthcoming marriage to Miriam as it concerned God's approval.

The two talked for nearly an hour before David recommended that they retire for the night. He was obviously moved by Reuben's disclosures and determined to visit the synagogue the following day to further search the Scriptures. Reuben asked to go with him. Each found it difficult to fall asleep that night while pondering the strange developments which were unfolding before their eyes.

Meanwhile, Miriam lay awake for a different reason. She wondered how she would get news to her dearest friend, Rebecca, in a remote part of Judea near Bethlehem. She wanted her to be an attendant at the wedding, along with Rhoda and two other young women from

Cana. I really should ask the daughter of Mary, Reuben's cousin from Nazareth, she thought, even though I don't know her. But if I did that, I would need to ask Deborah. Well, why not? She is betrothed, and I must get rid of that jealous feeling I have about her. It's pure foolishness! After all, Reuben loves me no matter what our families did to our lives. Tomorrow I'll talk to Mama about the girls.

"How can I get word to Rebecca to be my bridesmaid at my wedding, Mama?" Miriam asked Esther the following morning as they worked in the kitchen. "I know of no one going down into her area."

"Your father can ask when he meets with the other men in town this evening. We might even be fortunate enough to find a caravan going to Jerusalem. One of the temple priests could see that word got to her. I feel certain it can be arranged."

Miriam decided to ask Reuben about Deborah and Jesus' sister, whose name she did not know. There was often someone traveling to Nazareth, though not always a resident of Cana. She would not trust a Roman soldier to deliver a message. She would sooner trust a wayfarer.

"Oh, Mama, I hope I will look beautiful for Reuben. I want him to be proud of me!"

"My child, your beauty shines from within. That is something you cannot hide. But you will be properly adorned and you may wear some of my silver jewelry. I have chosen just the right flowers for your crown— some roses I have taken special care with. Jacob can clip the thorns before we weave them into the wreath for your head. You will be beautiful, dear one."

That evening by the well, Reuben gave Miriam a brief, tender kiss before revealing all he had heard and seen on his journey to Nazareth. She had planned to discuss the wedding with him but realized his mind was consumed with his journey to Nazareth. Of course, she was likewise anxious to hear the news. We have so much to talk about and so little time each day to do so, she complained to herself.

"Reuben, do you realize what you are telling me?" she exclaimed after hearing his story.

"Yes, my darling, I do. And I don't wonder about your astonishment—and maybe your doubts. I was the same way until I heard, saw and spoke with Jesus. Even speaking with Nathanael was equally convincing. Do you believe me at all?"

"Reuben, I would never doubt you. You know that. It's just…it's just that the whole thing is not as I imagined. And how could I ever convince Papa?"

"You may never convince him, Miriam. That's something we must consider and accept. Jesus will be coming to our wedding, you know, and there is always the chance your father will speak with him at the feast. But I have my own convictions, Miriam, and will not change them to suit your father. I hope you understand that," he told her gently but firmly, putting his hands on her shoulders and looking into her eyes.

"I understand, Reuben, and I only hope I can have the convictions you do. Bear with me, my love, until I can find out for myself. But right now, your word will do for me."

After a brief exchange about the wedding guests, they kissed and parted.

Will we always have so much to talk about? she wondered as she hastened to her home. At least we will have the nights together. The nights…

In spite of all the happiness infusing her soul, Miriam suddenly realized her wedding night would effect a great change in her life. Her status as a maiden would disappear. All modesty around Reuben would be snatched away, and he would know her as no one had since she had blossomed into young womanhood.

Fear inched itself into her mind, along with a certain amount of anxiety. Will I be able to go through with it? Will it hurt? What will actually happen? I want Reuben, but I'm afraid! Her heart beat faster with each burning thought and she wished she were a little girl again and could run to her mother for comfort. But she could not run to her mother now. These were things she did not feel comfortable discussing with Esther. They were too personal.

"Miriam, my dear," her mother had said to her one day as the two were examining the wedding garment, "do not fear your wedding night. Reuben is a gentle man and it will be all right."

But it was these very words which had brought on her misgivings. No one would ever talk about what would actually happen, and she wondered now why it would be necessary for Reuben to be gentle.

Preparations for the wedding caused the days to pass quickly for both households. Since Reuben and David had only begun the house the couple would live in, the bride and bridegroom would live temporarily with Reuben's family. Johhebed and Rhoda spent happy hours scrubbing down and whitewashing a small cubicle which would be the bridal chamber. A fresh pallet was made and covered with a piece of fine linen Johhebed had purchased months before in Jericho. A large urn was placed in one corner for holding flowers. David bought a straw mat for the floor, and Reuben watched impatiently for a caravan to come through so that he might find a suitable wedding gift for his bride. An ample dowry had already been given to Miriam the night of the marriage agreement.

The whole town had been invited to the wedding feast to be held at the home of David and Johhebed. Music makers had been engaged, and Reuben's wedding garment, once begun and then put away, was completed. Garments were also obtained for the guests.

Johhebed, Esther and Rhoda worked for days making sweet cakes enriched with dates, nuts and figs. Jacob was enlisted to crack the nuts. Fruits and cheeses were kept as cool as possible, and the dried fruits were kept away from nimble fingers so as to be available when needed.

David had chosen Jonas to act as steward for the wedding feast. Seeing that all went well for the week-long occasion was a big responsibility. Jonas was a responsible person and would serve David well.

Rebecca had been notified by way of a passing caravan, but Miriam would possibly not know until her wedding day whether or not her friend was coming. She could only hope.

Azariah, Rachel and Deborah had likewise been notified by one of the townsmen going to Magdala who had promised to give the message to one of the many fishermen from Capernaum.

Every possible detail had been considered, and it was hoped that nothing untoward would happen and that there would be ample food and wine at the feast.

The day of the wedding was now at hand. Miriam's friend, Rebecca, had arrived with a caravan the evening before, escorted by her older brother, Aaron. Azariah, Rachel, Deborah and Eleazar had been with Reuben and family for two days. The only persons missing were the cousins from Nazareth. The hour was early, however, so there was still time for their arrival.

Miriam was caught up in the excitement of her day of days. She and Rebecca were already beginning to arrange her hair. The crown of white roses would be her last adornment.

Esther's first concern, after feeding Nathan and Jacob, was to tidy up the house and rid it of every bit of excess dirt and disorder. The canopy for the bride and bridegroom was set up in the courtyard, and Esther placed her most beautiful plants on either side of it. She was grateful that her love of flowers was being put to such good use. Many of the neighbors brought what they could salvage at that time of year. Their home had never looked more beautiful. Esther herself was radiant with a glow of happiness for her daughter.

The old faded yellow cushions in the courtyard were replaced with new straw mats. Nathan obtained extra water jars for cleansing purposes.

He had gone to the synagogue to pray and speak with the rabbi, and both would return together in the afternoon. There was a certain heaviness in his heart, but the die had been cast and he must go along with the occasion.

Reuben was still awaiting the arrival of Nathanael. His three other friends from Cana—Aaron, Epher, and Iru—were already at his house, along with the sympathetic Eleazar, teasing him a bit and trying to alleviate his nervousness.

Tables were being set up by the servants along one wall of the courtyard, and these would hold the abundance of food which had been prepared. Reuben covered the floors with straw mats. He had obtained four stone water jugs, each of which held about twenty gallons of water, to sit beside the two the family kept by their doorway for purification rites. The roads were still dusty and many people would be coming. A great deal of water would be needed.

Reuben continued to glance anxiously down the road during the day for signs of Jesus and Nathanael. Mary and the rest of her family arrived around the sixth hour, profuse with apologies for being so late.

"James had to complete a plow which a farmer who refused to wait any longer had ordered some time ago," Mary explained to Johhebed. "Had it been Jesus, the plow would have been finished long ago, but Jesus has given up the carpenter shop," she added wistfully.

"Just as long as you came—that's what is important," smiled Johhebed, handing Mary and the others towels for the cleansing that was required after the journey. "I would appreciate your helping Jonas, our steward for the feast, to see that there is plenty of food and wine set out. I know I can depend upon you, Mary. My sister-in-law, Rachel, will help you if you need her, but she does not always take things seriously. Besides, she is caught up in preparations for her own daughter's wedding, so I would rather count on you."

"Of course, Johhebed. I told you I would be happy to assist in any way I could. We are planning to stay the whole week, now that James has caught up on his work. Has Jesus arrived? He sent word to me that he was coming."

"Not yet, Mary, but we do look for him. He told Reuben he would come. And Nathanael, who is with him, is to be one of Reuben's attendants.

At that moment she heard Reuben shout, "Here comes Jesus and Nathanael, and four other men are with them! Praise be to God!"

Reuben left the gate where he had been standing when he saw the party of travelers and rushed to greet them. He recognized Andrew and John, whom he had met on his trip to Nazareth, and Jesus introduced him to the two strangers, Simon Peter, brother of Andrew, and James, brother of John.

"It's a pleasure to have you as our guests," Reuben assured the men, "and Jesus, we're glad you could make it. Your family is already here and helping with the preparations."

Turning to Nathanael, Reuben inquired, "Where is Philip? I was hoping he could come also."

"He is preaching in another village. Someone has to bring the message to our people. Since Jesus was to be here, Philip accepted the challenge to speak in one of the synagogues and to any willing listeners this week. He sent his regrets and wishes you much happiness."

"I appreciate that," responded Reuben, "and now let us all go in and join the others. Rhoda!" he called to his sister. "Bring towels to our guests!" Pointing to the water jars, he bid them cleanse themselves. He noticed that the man named John washed the feet of Jesus. Is this another sign to consider? pondered Reuben.

The time was drawing near to go to Miriam's house and claim his dearest love as his bride. Taking

Nathanael with him, he ascended to his room to change into his wedding garment. It was carefully laid out on the pallet, along with the rest of his attire. His eyes sparkled as he viewed the blue and white striped robe, edged with a brilliant blue fringe on the hem and on the wide striped sash.

"I must say you are a handsome figure in that robe," voiced Nathanael, after Reuben had donned the garment. "With the crown of roses Esther made for you, you will look like a king!"

"I will feel like a king with Miriam as my bride," Reuben said enthusiastically. "Now to put on the gold chain, ring and bracelets Father loaned me. He wants me to keep the ring as a wedding gift. Miriam will wear the topaz ring I gave her as a gift.

"Am I fit now to claim my bride?" he asked, turning for Nathanael to see him.

"I only hope I will look half as good if I should decide to marry," assured Nathanael.

A shout of approval greeted Reuben as he came down the stairs into the crowded room. He was all but shoved through the door into the courtyard and out into the street. David and Johhebed were waiting for him at the gate, and it seemed as if the whole town was following him.

It was a time of great joy for everyone, but Reuben's joy knew no bounds. What will Miriam look like? I know she will be beautiful, but will she approve of me? Thoughts kept running through his head as he rounded the bend in the road which brought her house into view. Many people had gathered outside and cheered wildly as the groom and his procession appeared.

Reaching the courtyard, Reuben, David, Johhebed, and the four attendants entered, leaving the others waiting in the road for the bride and bridegroom to appear as man and wife. A wedding was Cana's most joyful occasion, and all but the most necessary work ceased, as it did on holy days. The Jews considered a marriage to be more than happy, it was sacred, as they felt God intended it to be.

Suddenly Reuben stopped and looked behind him. There was one person he wanted to be with him, and he searched the crowd to find that one person. At the perimeter of the group, he saw him standing to one side alone. Jesus. Reuben caught his eye and beckoned for him to come. For some reason, the excited onlookers calmed down and made way for the carpenter from Nazareth to join Reuben. They entered the house with the rest of the wedding party and Reuben's parents.

Inside the atmosphere was charged with the joy of the occasion. The bridesmaids giggled with the anticipation and self-consciousness of youth. Miriam was radiant, dressed in her white linen gown, finely embroidered on the bottom by her own fingers. She wore her mother's silver chain holding a medallion, and her head was covered with a sheer veil of white, draped under her chin with the ends falling to the back. A crown of white roses, matching the one Reuben wore, reposed on top of the veil. Her face was covered with the veil, with the exception of her eyes.

Reuben stopped still when he saw his bride. He was charged with a spiritual feeling, believing God was giving him a very special gift, to love and endear forever. "Hallel! Hallel!" he burst forth before going to embrace the parents of Miriam.

Nathan was the only solemn person in the room. His eyes were misty, and he stood with head bowed and feet wide apart, hands behind his back. As Reuben softly whispered, "Thank you," to him, he accepted the embrace graciously but without enthusiasm.

Esther, who was tastefully, but simply gowned, welcomed Reuben and the others warmly. She was obvious in her attempts to make the others comfortable and see to the details of the occasion.

Jacob hung by the gate ready to fire the torches which would light the way for the procession to proceed to the wedding feast. His eyes rested on his little friend, Naomi, in the crowd, and he was reminded of what his sister had said to him. Immediately, he turned the other way, disgusted that he would even remember such a thing.

Standing under the canopy the couple received the blessings of their parents, the rabbi, and at Reuben's request, Jesus of Nazareth. Tears blinded the eyes of Miriam and Reuben as they were swept out to the road and covered with the canopy carried by the groomsmen. Jacob and Eleazar carried the torches and the crowd fell in behind to form a procession to Reuben's home—now Miriam's home also. Psalms were sung, and a long route was taken so as to pass by the homes of those who were unable to come because of illness or some other reason. These people all shouted well wishes to the bride and groom, including wishes for many children. Miriam and Reuben could only remain silent, as the noise of the crowd singing and shouting precluded any reasonable conversation. However, it was not necessary. They floated on a cloud of sheer ecstasy and talk would have been superfluous.

Servants at the house greeted the procession as it arrived, handing out fresh towels and bidding everyone enter. Johhebed, Esther, Deborah and Rachel saw to the comfort of the guests, and Jonas and Mary gave a last-minute check to the bounty of delicacies on the tables against the wall. Johhebed was grateful for the colorful materials she had bought in Jericho, as they made suitable cloths for the tables. She planned to wash them later and use them for something else.

The bride and bridegroom were seated in the center of the room and given the first tastes of the food and wine. Numerous wine cups were raised to their health, long life, abundance and children. The usual wishes for a son were proclaimed.

Reuben often cast his eyes at Jesus who had entered into the merrymaking with ease and pleasure. Reuben secretly hoped he and Nathan would talk sometime during the week. If Nathan were only more open minded!

A week, a whole week, Reuben considered. Miriam and I will have precious little time alone during that time...except at night. No one will bother us then. In fact, it is night now. Why couldn't we...?

He started to whisper something to Miriam, but he needn't have made the attempt. His parents and Esther were already making hints that it was time for the couple to retire to the bridal chamber. Blushing, Reuben helped Miriam, also blushing, up from her mat and led her upstairs to the small cubicle which had been prepared for them. Well wishers called out remarks to them, but they hastened their retreat. Misgivings all but overcame Miriam for a moment, but her supreme happiness pushed them away.

The transition from maidenhood to fulfilled womanhood was accomplished beautifully and easily through the love and gentle ministrations of Reuben. As the couple found themselves alone in their bridal chamber, fragrant with the blossoms placed there by Rhoda and Rebecca, their first impulse was to come together in an embrace. How good it was to be away from the people!

Reuben eagerly ran his hands through her thick hair, removing the circlet of flowers and veil as he eagerly kissed her willing lips.

"You are mine forever, dearest one," he whispered in her ear, "my wife."

"Yes, Reuben," she answered softly, "and you are my wonderful husband at last. Oh! I can hardly believe it!"

As they clung tightly to each other, Reuben gradually and gently removed her garment, caressing her at the same time to take away any embarrassment that might be present. As he picked her up and laid her on their wedding couch, she continued to cling to him.

Longing turned into fierce desire, and all traces of fear dissolved as she succumbed to Reuben's love and gentleness. The slight stab of pain was obscured by pure ecstasy, and they were one flesh at last, just as God intended. The moment was sacred and beautiful. Miriam could scarcely believe the joy she felt in the arms of this tender and loving young man, the one for whom she had saved herself.

The evidence of her virginity would be there for the prying eyes of family members, but she did not care. All that mattered was the love and happiness of this moment.

The week was half over when Mary made a disarming discovery. The wine supply had run out, even though Jonas had taken special care to see that there was enough. But there have been extra guests, she reasoned. Jesus himself brought along four friends we hadn't counted on. Certainly no one has gotten drunk or disorderly. It must be the extra people.

Calling Jesus aside, she said, "They have no wine."

"Woman, what have I to do with you?" he replied gently. "My hour is not yet come."

Mary understood his meaning and turned to the servants. "Whatever he says to you, do it." They looked puzzled, as they did not know this man and had not been told that he would be assisting in any way.

"Fill the water pots with fresh water," he commanded them.

They emptied the heavy pots which had been used for cleansing and filled them with fresh water from the well down the road, grumbling at such an unnecessary task. There was still plenty of water in them for ordinary use.

Returning to the house, they set the pots down at the usual place and told Jesus it had been done. Their lips curled and eyes squinted as they glanced at one another to silently complain of this extra burden.

Seeing their malcontent, he said to them, "Draw out now, and bear it unto the steward of the feast."

In shock, they saw the color of the liquid they drew out. It was no longer clear water. It was red…the color of wine. It even had the smell of wine. The frightened and befuddled servants did as they were told and took a portion to Jonas, not daring to tell him what had actually happened. Not knowing the source of this supply, he was pleased to receive it and proceeded to taste it before giving it to the guests.

Delighted with the taste of the wine, Jonas beckoned to Reuben and told him that every man sets out his best wine at the beginning of a feast, so that when the guests have drunk freely he may bring out that which is not as good.

"But you have kept your good wine until now. A most unusual thing, Reuben. Mmmm...it is superb!"

"But Jonas," exclaimed the puzzled Reuben, "I happen to know that we had no more wine. I was with Father when we got it out. Exactly, where did this come from? Find out from the servants and let me know, please. If one of our guests has provided some we must thank him."

A few moments later, Jonas excitedly returned to Reuben with the story about what had actually happened. "Surely they are making this up," said Jonas. "Such a thing could not be true. I will seek out Mary and ask her about it."

But Reuben believed the story. He took Nathanael aside and told him, just to confirm what was convicting him. "With God all things are possible," said Nathanael. "I do not doubt this one bit." Turning to the boisterous but happy man beside him—the one named Simon Peter—he spoke for a moment in low tones to him, receiving a nod of approval from the fisherman.

"He, too, believes it," said Nathanael to Reuben, who by now was in a shocked state. He had never heard of anything like this. For it to happen at his own wedding feast was almost inconceivable, if it had not been for the presence of the one he was convinced by now was the Messiah, the long-awaited one.

Late that night as he lay with Miriam in his arms, he told her about the strange and miraculous happening. She sat straight up in bed with her eyes wide with wonder and astonishment.

"Oh, Reuben! I said I would never doubt you, and I do not now. How blessed we are that God has sent the Messiah into our very home, to our wedding feast, and he performed a miracle, possibly his first, right in our courtyard. What a wonderful way for us to begin our life together, Reuben…my love."

"We will follow his teaching and his very life," Reuben assured her, pulling her down once more into the comfort of his embrace. Perhaps your father in time will also believe."

"I pray he will," she whispered, stroking his thick hair and placing her head upon his shoulder. "I love you, Reuben," she told him tenderly. "I want to make you a good wife."

"You will, little one whom I love so much…and you will be a good mother to our children." He kissed her long and tenderly.

Meanwhile, downstairs, David slyly watched as Nathan reluctantly talked with the carpenter from Nazareth.

To order additional copies of

THE WEDDING

please send $10.99
plus $3.95 shipping and handling to:

Marion C. Beavers
Magnolia Manor South #131
3011 East-By-Pass
Moultrie, GA 31769

*Quantity Discounts are Available

To order by phone,
have your credit card ready and call

1-800-917-BOOK